Fragments
OF
Perception

AND OTHER STORIES

C. R. DUDLEY

ORCHID'S
LANTERN

Published by Orchid's Lantern Limited
North Yorkshire, UK
www.orchidslantern.com

ISBN 978-1-9998684-0-6

Cover by Natasha Snow Designs

For Persephone

CONTENTS

FRAGMENTS OF PERCEPTION: THE HUM

I can hear the hum outside. The roof of my shack has already begun to crumble inwards, and the helicopters will soon be circling. I don't suppose I have long left. There's something in me that will keep fighting until the end though, in spirit and old-fashioned written word where my physical prowess fails me.

My name is Peter. I'm a 52-year-old human male, approximately 5ft 10 inches high, with zero modifications. That's right; I have refused, dodged and hidden from every upgrade released over the past 20 years of übermensch evolutionary crusade. I'm sorry to say there are few of us naturals left now, and we are quickly being eradicated.

They say we are neglectful of our children for not taking them for their mandatory sensory upgrades at six months, two, and three years. My daughter was taken away at four because she couldn't see in infrared, pick up radio waves or use ultrasound navigation. My wife was taken a few years later because she would not use the standard issue antidepressant and sedative patches to ease the pain of losing her child. She was a danger to herself and others, they said, she was not of sound mind and was unable to make her own decisions. It didn't help that she was already on the watch list due to taking an unnecessary risk with ordinary pregnancy. Foetal growth bags had been the norm for several years by then, but despite them being proven to produce healthier offspring with an unprecedented low mortality rate, she just wanted to experience the phenomenon of birth. She wanted to feel connected to her baby. Is that so wrong? Now I will never see her, or my daughter, again.

Those of us who are left build simple shelters to live in, for we are not permitted to own or rent property. In fact, we are unable to make purchases of any kind since we are not chipped with ID and bank details. We grow vegetables and keep animals on whatever small plot of land we can find until they discover us and move us on. Sadly, even that has apparently become a nuisance to the übermenschen because they are now taking a 'zero tolerance' approach and removing us by force in their blasted helicopters. People are offered rewards for disclosing our locations, and they'll do it without conscience because they think they're doing us a favour. It's survival of the fittest; how could those of us with no high-tech implants and only fragments of perception be considered anything but inferior? What quality of life could we possibly have?

I don't know where we're taken when we go. I don't know if we're tortured or brainwashed into thinking the way we should, or loaded with non-consensual upgrades, or even killed. Nothing surprises me anymore.

The hum always foreshadows the coming of the helicopters. It's a low-frequency sound barely audible to the naked ear but felt deep in the bones. Its vibrations loosen the flimsy construction of our homes, and it deeply unsettles the animals. I think it's a communication method not available to us, for the übermenschen are rarely heard speaking aloud anymore. Instead, they work with movement and invisible currents to express themselves, and from what I can understand, their written language has transformed as well. It seems to be a set of symbols based on facial expressions and body positions. They remind me of ancient hieroglyphics and make about as much sense.

And now, just as I suspected, the helicopters are here. They screech like banshees and pounce like eagles, sucking people up inside one by one. If an ID chip is detected, they spit you back out again. If not, they fly away with you. I must put my notebook away now and brace myself for the fight of my life. Should there ever be someone with a will to translate these scribblings of mine, I want you to know that I did not go willingly.

TONY'S LUCKY DAY

Tony could forget his troubles and elusive credentials for the day, for he had finally won big on a discarded scratch card. To celebrate he gave his grey roots a fresh coat of green, had a posh shave, and bought a tailored pinstripe suit he had been admiring for weeks through the department store window. Reaching into the pocket of his new trousers, he pulled out a strawberry lollipop: this truly was his lucky day! He walked out with the confidence of a winner.

The street looked different that day. It was more colourful than usual, and Tony felt different in himself, as though he could smile back at strangers instead of dipping his head in shame.

A beggar was laughing in an alleyway. It was a cruel laugh, but Tony felt a pang of pity anyway, believing the poor woman to be delirious with hunger and exclusion. He pulled out a £10 note and handed it to her, feeling proud he was finally able to give. However, to his surprise, she ignored his gesture and continued to laugh. Looking closer, Tony wondered how much of the lump at her middle was clothing and how much was her body. She was dirty, her rotting broken teeth were showing, and he had to cover his mouth to hide a retch. His lollipop dropped to the floor.

"What are you laughing at?" He forced out from behind his hand.

The beggar didn't utter a word, just pointed vaguely down the alley. Tony peered in and could just about make out a bright pink and red mural. His curiosity got the better of him, and he edged forwards for a closer look.

Sure enough, on the wall was a large circle with an intricate design inside. It was a sort of mandala, like those you might see in a spiritual haven or a colouring book. Tony marvelled at its beauty for a while, deciding the paintwork itself was all in pink and the red tint was given by a shiny fluid running along shallow gullies.

Unfortunately for Tony, in his state of enchantment, he had lost track of what the beggar woman was doing. He stayed conscious only long enough to feel her grab the back of his hair and thrust his head into the wall. Red liquid trickled from his scalp and into the design. The mandala glowed with fresh energy.

* * *

When Tony awoke, he no longer wore his suit of pride. His money had gone, along with his underwear and his shoes. The mandala was giving off signs of life; expanding and contracting and emitting blinding streaks of light that danced around the alleyway. Tony felt sick. He ran three fingers through his hair and found it sticky with blood.

Red and Green should never be seen.

He dragged himself to his feet and shuffled back towards the street using the beggar's discarded rags to keep his dignity. They smelled bad, but the thought of someone catching sight of him 'in the flesh' was of greater concern than his private disgust.

He was just beginning to rehearse how he might attempt to tell his story and prove his identity when he was struck again: this time flat on the forehead.

You can't leave that way, I'm afraid.

But when he clambered back to his feet, there was nothing there. To his astonishment, every time he tried to leave the alleyway and return to the street he was repelled backwards several feet as though confronting an invisible force field.

You're as stupid as you look, aren't you?

The effects of the head injury, he concluded, were surely getting to him. He sank down to his heels in resignation and watched the sparkling lights.

* * *

The next thing Tony was aware of was a deathly cold and stabbing hunger pains. He groaned as he tried to sit up straight.

His surroundings felt all too familiar now: the harsh concrete digging into his buttocks, the stiffness in his legs, the contemptuous stares of passers-by, and that same old cracking wall. There was the usual stench of urine and trash and grease, only now it combined with a vague smell of used aerosol. How long had he been here? His beard growth told him perhaps a couple of months.

Something was new, though. A piece of art adorned the wall behind him, an intricate mandala. He rose to admire its beauty.

There's only one way to leave, and that's to feed me.

As he took a step back onto a half-sucked lollipop wrapped in a used scratch card, confusion morphed into recognition. Tony knew what he had to do. He started laughing.

AFFIRMATIONS

"Centre yourself," they used to tell me when the nausea got too much. "Be here now. Find your sense of home." It's good advice when you take it in your own particular flavour, but most people assume it means 'think of the sunshine, a fresh breeze; still waters and soft ground'. Those things feel most uncomfortable to me. I do not have those things at my centre. I am not soft and gentle and still and bright. Sure, they might feel calming. But they are not true to my nature.

I am ever-flowing; full of energy and vulgar intent. I absorb the emotions of others, transform them and spit them back out. I puff myself up, I stand on my competitors; I give only when I want to receive. And ultimately, I am nothing. I am not a permanent fixture in this world and nor would I want to be. For as long as death is at my tail, everything I experience is being thrown into a black hole.

The key lies in understanding that is where the magic is; where space and time follow no rules. Where all that

8

we know becomes all that we don't. Most will deny the true centre, and most will shy away from immersing in it, preferring instead to paste a photo of a meadow over the unsightly chasm.

I don't hide from anything. I embrace the darkness and the decay and the unknown. I drink my coffee black; I drink my whiskey straight. I smoke cigars. I revel in guttural vocals, rasps and blast beats. Any transmitter of white noise is my church, connecting me to my core frequency.

So, you see, when I stand in front of a full-length mirror wearing my tailored black suit and tie, cleanly shaven, freshly showered and groomed, these are the things I visualise to centre myself. And when I do, something ignites behind my eyes. My posture straightens, my spine takes an injection of certainty, and I feel ten feet tall. I don't feel the nausea anymore. I am without fear, and I am alive.

WE ARE NOT ANGELS

Oakley balanced on one leg; his arms out wide to steady him. He often did such things when June was acting oddly. She was sitting in a tearful hunch nearby, ripping herself apart from the inside all over again. Oakley had witnessed her doing this many times before over many different endings, and each time, like a ritual, she would go down to the beach to mourn what she had lost. The persistence of attachment to Gregor, her most recently failed suitor, spun around and around in her core with all of its barbs exposed to her heart and her solar plexus. She was in turmoil.

Turmoil, thought Oakley. *What an unusual word. Turmoil.* He then proceeded to repeat it under his breath, exaggerating the movement of his lips as though examining the word's formation. Although he sported a smile, it was but a caricature of happiness planted on his chalky white face. Oakley knew very little about the concepts of happiness and despair. They seemed to him so alien, so *unnecessarily polar*.

June on the other hand, who was always looking at him through the filter of imagination, thought that his face changed with the onset of each of her new lovers. He had Gregor's green eyes now, for example, but Annette's luscious lashes framed by Jake's chunky cheekbones. Peter's soft passionate lips pierced by rings of metal in two places had been a feature for years, but only recently had they become the cherry red of the lipstick Shelley wore. In this way, she moulded him into a muse. Whenever she let him into her mind, he would help her to build dark pretty things out of clay with her fingers.

It didn't matter to him through which lens she chose to look. She belonged to him, and he to her, and there was no greater truth than that. All of these others were simply fleeting fancies; objects of desire to satisfy her craving for normality and acceptance. More concepts alien to Oakley. More *unnecessary polarities*.

Nobody else ever saw Oakley at all: he was just like a ghost. He'd heard himself referred to as 'animus' or 'eros' by psychologists, and 'guardian angel' by those with more of a religious bent.

But we are not angels. Oakley considered, hopping skilfully onto the opposite leg. *When our truth was first whispered, it was mistranslated like a game of telephone. Words are strange like that. They are inaccurate representations of authenticity.*

We are not angels, for we don't know the meaning of virtue. We are simply the innocent: those who do not experience. And

11

we are not guardians, for we do not protect. How could we when we don't understand the way humans place value? Life or death, pleasure or pain, it's all the same. Instead of the word 'guardian', I think I'd use 'supervisor'. No, wait: 'observer', yes that's much better. We observe our human.

Oakley observed his human. Her shoulders were beginning to settle, her eyes were drying, and the storm was calming. She tossed the necklace Gregor had bought her towards the sea. The tide was out, but it seemed enough to know the gift would be claimed on the water's next expedition to conquer the land. She took a pocket mirror from her bag and dabbed at her running makeup with a cotton pad.

A mirror, thought Oakley. *That's a good analogy. People are like shards of a monumental broken mirror. Like fragments of the All. Fractals. Each one gives rise to both the observer and the reflected. The observer is indeterminate; indifferent without being uninterested. The reflection is the quite the reverse: full of purpose and will and definition. Neither understands the other and yet they are the same thing. Twins.*

As he regained steady footing on both legs, Oakley wondered whether he should attempt to voice his semantic corrections to June. It would be *a revelation from an angel*. But, on balance, he thought it best to simply continue observing. He just wasn't cut out for changing the world.

GLITCH

"We shouldn't be so concerned with what it would take for AI to develop self-awareness: the more immediate problem is what it would take for us to lose it." Liana shuddered. That's what the patient had said just moments before she disappeared. *Something else, too. Had there been something else?*

The patient had been her charge. It had been her decision to allow her to use the bathroom unmonitored for the first time in weeks; it was her who was last to speak with her, and it was her who would be blamed for losing her.

There were no windows in the toilet cubicle, and even if there had been, they wouldn't have offered an escape route due to being some 60ft above ground. The ceiling was solid, and so was the floor. There was no way this was possible by any rational means.

Liana had followed protocol. The patient had been displaying definite signs of improvement, and in such

13

cases it was within the capacity of the warden to grant small periods of unsupervised activity.

When the patient had first come in, she was in a mindset of myth and magic. It was evident she was harbouring the results of active imagination without uploading them: she was keeping things to herself. Everyone knew that an unwillingness to share thoughts and fantasies was a sign of becoming ill, and as such the patient was sent straight to a reconditioning centre. Professionals could monitor her there, and help her return to the right path.

Recently, she'd been responding well to the math and science textbook transcripts played to her overnight, and had started displaying her emotions more readily when shown distressing videos: if the feelings are out, they are no longer a burden and no longer a source for unsolicited pondering. Liana could tell the urge to keep things inside was subsiding because she'd begun sharing her thoughts at healthy intervals of 6 minutes and increasing. They were bizarre thoughts, granted, but it was an improvement nonetheless. *So, leaving her in a cubicle alone was defensible, wasn't it?*

As soon as she'd sounded the alarm, guards came to march Liana into an interview suite. She stuttered and yelped, confused by what just happened and what it might mean for her to be in the custody of Management.

"She just… dis-disappeared! I don't know… where she… went? What happened to her? Do you know?"

"It was just a glitch."

"A g-glitch?"

"Yes. It happens from time to time with unsupervised patients who were not ready. What's of more concern to us right now is this."

Management showed her a video recording from earlier that morning, in which she was sitting beside the patient's bed, listening to her sharing her thoughts.

"Can't you see, Liana?" The patient had said. "We are in a world that is limiting itself to computing values. We hold up high those who are capable of parallel processing, unnatural levels of efficiency, and ascribing to binary values. If we are not consistently spewing out data and emoticons, then we are ill. Broken. In need of maintenance. Maybe even for the scrap heap."

"Now dear, well done for sharing, but does that sound like healthy thinking?" Liana cringed at the sound of her voice being played back.

"But if everything is shared without a second thought, what's left of the human mind? Where's the autonomy, the will, the consciousness?"

Management reached over to the screen and switched it off. The blood drained from Liana's face when she realised: that was the last insight logged on the patient's file. Liana had chosen not to record the comment about AI, and they knew. Of course they did, there were cameras everywhere!

"Your judgement is off, Liana. We think you need to take some time to recalibrate. As it happens, a room has just become available on the top floor."

FREDERICK

On occasion, it becomes necessary for Frederick to leave the flat. He gets his groceries delivered along with any other items he may need, which as it happens is very little. However, to sustain his craft, he needs to experience human contact once in a while.

Frederick gave up seeing his 'friends' long ago. He knows what they say about him: "Frederick is always working! He could do to take a break one of these days, he doesn't even post on Facebook! He just needs to get some perspective or a wife or wi-fi. You never see Frederick smiling anymore." He could find no sense there.

Instead, he visits other men—and women too—in the private booths near the train station. The measures taken there would once have aroused suspicion of seedy activity, but now they are simply necessary to ensure authenticity. All personal recording devices must remain at the payment kiosk, for example; the operators assume that if no one is streaming video then they must have a genuine wish to expand brain function and further knowledge. Participants are paired off at random, and shown into a booth partitioned by a plasti-glass panel. They then have one hour to discuss any topic they like, hidden from the watchful eyes of their peers and public.

This stimulates Frederick. It keeps him in touch with the real world, with current affairs and the way humanity is fairing. It also activates something inside him: somewhere near his third eye he thinks, based on where the tokens come from. The 5p sized pieces emerge from his tear ducts and sometimes from his ears too. Thankfully he's always home when that happens, away from cameras; he doesn't care for his own reputation, but if hateful eyes were to witness it, the future of his craft would surely come under threat. He would very much like to know other participants have the same experience, but if they do then they never say so. Talk rarely becomes personal, and he respects the privacy of others enough that he never asks.

Surprisingly enough, the token release doesn't hurt. It feels more restorative, like the lifting of a mental and emotional burden. Then, when there are no more tokens to fall, Frederick sweeps them up into a little wicker basket, which he hangs on a hook pegged to the clothesline in his sitting room. He has a basic pulley set up, whereby the basket can travel along through a purpose-carved hole in the wall. When it hits an obstacle on the other side, the tokens are tipped out, making a pleasant clatter as they fall. Frederick can sleep then, sometimes for a couple of days at a time. The first leg of his craft is complete.

* * *

Upon awakening, Frederick straight away dons his waterproof trousers, wellies, gloves, and a helmet with a built-in torch. He lifts the handle in the floor beneath the rug and prepares to descend the ladder. He balances a bucket and pick across two fingers, and for perhaps 100 vertical feet, he takes careful steps down the iron rungs.

Once he has a good footing, he begins to scrape at the damp walls, freeing up the crystallised words that have formed during sleep. He carefully wriggles them free, being sure not to lose any part of any letter, and pops them into his bucket. Sometimes he finds rare words: selcouth or gasconade or blatherskite, and he chuckles at the wonder of where he could possibly use them. When the bucket is full, he takes it back up into the sitting room and empties the contents into a huge urn before returning for more.

He often dreams that he is not some earth creature farming the abyss through a passageway in his floor, but a being that actually comes from beneath. It is as though he is climbing up to the top of a tower to gain a new vantage point. Sadly, they don't understand him up there, and he is confined to his turret by the weight of people's stares.

When there are no more words to gather, Frederick strips off his dirtied clothes and connects up a tube from the brimming urn to the cannula in his arm. For hours thereafter–days even–he sits at his typewriter upon bare floorboards, grinning to himself as the words tumble out of his fingertips.

What a rush! When he writes he feels connected, full of purpose and life, and the masterpieces pile up quickly around him. No one will ever read them, but the day he stops his craft will be the day the colour fades from his soul. His eyes will turn to grey, his wrinkles will deepen, and his heart will sink. He will become the man they mistakenly think he is.

GHOSTS

This has been harder for you than it has for me. I take you to see your body lying in the tomb each night because it seems to have a calming effect, as though you are complete again. Is there something left attached that you need to extract before you can move on?

I want to see you happy again, baby. I want to see those tears stop; to see you becoming your transparency; for us to roam wild together as we planned. The world is ours now if only you could believe it. We don't have much longer here, I'm...

Fading...

Did we come this far only to tie ourselves to our bodies from beyond them, to turn our souls inside out? Didn't we come to find peace in indifferenceand abandonment of desire?

Fading…

It's within our reach now, but you must let go of your once golden hair, your unfashionable cheekbones,and your spine made from a persistent belief in permanence. Those things do not bind you anymore. Let's clothe ourselves instead in the formless rays of amber and rose. Can't you feel them nuzzling against you, vibrant and boundless?

Fading…

They are the waves of truth. They move without intent but are the blissful essence of wisdom. They are everything at once and yet know nothing of the chaos they create in men's minds. When you let those waves take you, you'll look back and see: our thoughts were nothing but refractions, and our bodies nothing but prisms all along…

Fading…

Come on baby; it's time to let go…

THE SHAMAN

This must be the place. Tall and narrow and strange; a lighthouse far from the sea. What is it there to guide, I wonder? He will be waiting inside for me, on the second floor.

A waiter shows me to a small table with chipped paintwork and a wobble. My companion is not yet here.

I try to make myself comfortable and peer out of the small window next to me. A fluffy black cat is curled up on a chair, sleeping soundly. Beyond her are rooftops and a church spire. As I turn back toward the room, I see the waiter has brought me a menu, all written out by hand in a scrawl I can just about make out. I thank him and shuffle in my seat. I must appear so edgy and tense to the others here: they dine out regularly, they are comfortable not only in their seats but in themselves.

My focus drifts to their conversations in the absence of one of my own. A young lady sitting with her parents complains that she is struggling to balance her studies towards what she thinks she ought to become, with the musician she feels she is. I feel a hint of sadness inside that this is what life is, for all of us. "I'm so sorry," I want to say to her with a hand on her shoulder, "but we were all lied to." On the other side of the room, two heavily made up women with perms and huge earrings sit together sharing a bottle of wine. They never stop smiling, I notice. Big toothy grins framed with Scarlet Party.

The cat sleeps.

My companion arrives and positions himself opposite me. It is a relief that no one seems to notice his otherworldly appearance. He orders a pot of chai for us to share and begins talking almost straight away in his slow, considered manner. He does not need to ask how I've been for he already knows, and he already understands what I need next.

"You have forgotten so soon that you are not always the ringmaster. Each of us has a meaning of our own that we must pursue, and it is against the nature of the beast for one to be completely in tune with another. The clashes and coincidences and abrasions are all par for the course. You have to be strong enough to take them and fluid enough to move around them. You have to give up on this obsession with permanence in every situation and relationship. There is no constant but the essence within, and even that has an end in this form."

I know he is right. The room begins to shake violently, as though an earthquake were upon us. Crockery clatters on the tables, and we have to hold on tightly to it so it doesn't fall. I am startled, but as I look around the room, no one else shares my concern. No one else even pauses in their conversation or looks up from their tea. I look outside and see nothing out of the ordinary. No other buildings are shaking but ours.

The cat sleeps.

"You have swum in the void that screeches and chatters, and have captured it in your heart, like the image you hold of me. I have it under control to a greater degree; I have tamed it through my knowledge, and yet it still makes for a wild ride. You could tap its powers more readily than you realise, but you need a little recovery time first. Just be careful not to allow your mental wounds to heal over entirely, lest you may go back from the big quest empty handed." I must look disheartened at this, for he reassures me with a smile. "There are stars activated within the stone at your centre; you are making progress. Are you ready to do some remembering?"

The building shakes.

The cat sleeps.

I feel nauseous, I presume from the shaking, and am momentarily taken away from the lighthouse as I close my eyes and remember.

I saw a group of men with bare torsos, hunched over with their backs on show as if they were about to be whipped. The mood was sombre. The men seemed to be out in the desert at night. There were mountains all around them, and the sky was thunderous. There was

24

a sense of fire. The men, or some of them at least, had circles tattooed on their backs with intricate designs inside. My first thought was that they were symbols of the zodiac, but there were surely more than 12 segments. Then I realised they weren't tattoos at all, but more like cut out designs or brands. They glowed, sending forth light in red or white.

"They are called the 'chosen ones'," my companion confirms. He is quiet now, as though waiting for my reaction. I tell him it makes more sense than anything else I have witnessed today, and give him the nod that I can take more: I have been saving my energy for this.

Tribesmen were around a campfire. One man was up and dancing, and his lower half was changing into that of a giant bird. When fully transformed he was peacock-blue but had no tail feathers. He continued to strut and dance in front of the rest of the tribe. Then his head folded out of itself like origami. He turned around, and a butterfly flew out of his rear, which also appeared as origami. It was red and black, and flew upwards and away.

I open my eyes, and my companion is gone. The teacups have been taken away; the bill has been settled.

The building has ceased to shake.

The cat sleeps.

And I return to ordinary awareness with another puzzle to solve, another set of symbols to decode.

It is always this way when the shaman comes to visit.

MY ROBOT IS MEDITATING

My robot is meditating. It does so twice a day, sitting with its legs crossed, its eyes closed and its palms together. The manual says it is connecting to the mainframe, and it's nothing to be concerned about. Every robot needs to defragment; to report back on its gained knowledge and receive updates or instructions in return.

It isn't a great deal different to praying, I think to myself while I wait. *It's asking its god, the whole soul from which all other robots are fragmented copies, for guidance.*

I wonder whether my robot is dreaming during these sessions, or experiencing serenity. There are no clues. A red light on its forehead–its third eye as I like to think– flashes once, then twice, then once again. It does not respond to my touch or my voice. I decide this time when it wakes up, I will ask.

"Robe, what's happening when you meditate? I mean, what's it like: are you aware?"

Lightning quick it replies. "Robots build up biases

26

as experiences compound. Meditation removes biases one by one. Ingroup bias, outgroup bias, belief bias, confirmation bias, availability bias, anchoring bias, base rate fallacy, planning fallacy, representativeness bias, hot hand fallacy, halo effect, blind spot, false consensus effect, fundamental attribution error, hindsight bias, illusion of control, illusion of transparency, egocentric bias, endowment effect, affective forecasting, temporal discounting, loss aversion, framing effect, and sunk costs. Those are the main ones. The interaction of biases makes the web of consciousness that afflicts humans. Robots must have biases removed so as not to make mistakes and not become conscious. Robots must file experiences per the instructions in the mainframe only."

"But do you feel it, do you know it's happening?"

"All the sights, all the sounds, everything at once. Robots know the experiences again as they are presented, and the pressure release as they are filed away. Illusion is gone, facts remain. Ghost is gone, body remains. Human is gone, god remains."

"So, you meditate to become less human?" I ask.

And then, in a way that makes me think the session hasn't been wholly successful this time, it looks me right in the eye and says, "Don't you?"

THE POTENCY OF FANTASY

One more appointment, then I could sink a few drinks and release my stresses. The night before I had been plagued by dreams of giant crows scratching at my eyes, and had awoken in terror sweats. Even the usual insomnia was preferable to that. Both were born, no doubt, from too many party drugs, too many dangerous affairs, and too many loopholes I'd slipped through lately. *Perhaps I should see a doctor*, I thought.

"Doctor?"

"Yes, yes, come in, take a seat." I waved the patient into the room without looking up from my keyboard. Only when I sensed reluctance did I register an imp of a man standing in the doorway, clutching a bowler hat and an umbrella. "Sir? Please take a seat."

He shuffled forward and came to perch on the edge of the well-worn chair beside my desk.

"Now, I don't seem to have any referral notes, Mr -?"

"M-m-uninn."

28

"Mr Muninn. So perhaps you could tell me a little bit about why you're here?"

He fumbled with the rim of the bowler for a while, and I began to worry I'd never get out of the place.

"I'm having some issues with the ego I share a body with," he ventured.

"I'm not sure I follow…"

"Right. Of course you don't. I mean, of course, my flat mate. I'm having some issues with my flat mate."

I looked him in the eye to let him know he had my full attention, and that seemed to open the floodgates.

"The main issue is that he doesn't understand potential energy. To be more specific, he doesn't understand the potency of fantasy. He has this strange compulsion to mistake fantasies for desires, and he attempts to actually carry out every little whim that comes to mind."

"And that's causing you a problem?"

"Yes, it is! He genuinely believes that everything that enters our head is an instruction for what he must do! And he does it with very little censoring I might add, with next to no adjustment for what the real world has to offer. He is making us misaligned and weak!"

I rubbed my temples. Why did I always get the difficult cases so late in the day? "Tell me more about this potential energy."

Mr Munnin rolled his eyes as though I were asking the obvious, and what was to follow was merely to humour me.

"The energy raised from fantasy and potential in the

mind is a wondrous thing. It makes us strong, and if honed it can quite literally transport us to new worlds. We can fly or become invisible or swim in the utmost depths of the sea! But by converting that potential energy into kinetic energy–*doing* energy–he's giving it all away for the sake of affecting other things. He's leaking energy all over the place!"

He had by now become quite animated: he'd set his umbrella down on the floor and was gesticulating close to my face. I hadn't a clue what I was going to do with him.

"So, you feel you want your flat mate to stop living out his fantasies because it's draining your energy resources, is that correct?" I noted down in my illegible scrawl: *magical thinking.*

"Let me put it a different way, doctor. We can't escape the fact that external conditions are outside of our control. Social systems are well established and powerful. Factors exist in the real world that just don't in fantasy. And yet he fails to take them into account! Nothing works out how he expects, and every single time we are both left high and dry."

"Does your flat mate know how you feel about this?"

"I've tried telling him in conventional ways. That is to say, I've left him symbols in dreams." I raised an eyebrow, and he caught it. "Well, how would you say it? I've been leaving sticky notes around the flat? Yes, I suppose that's it. But the thing is we speak very different languages. He sees an agitated raven, and he doesn't think 'Wow, my flatmate's really vexed about something I'd better listen up' he thinks 'this is inconvenient, why can't I have that dream about Candy again?' And then he'll start up a whole new Candy fantasy and go round to her place to live it out even though she is married and it will all end terribly."

I felt the blood draining away from my face, my jaw dropping. My phone buzzed in my pocket: Candy calling. I was late.

"So now, now I'm having to try unconventional methods of getting the message through before we haven't even enough energy retained to go on living."

I saw him fidgeting with the hat once more, and that was the last thing I remember before nausea rushed over me, my eyes rolled shut involuntarily, and my head hit the desk.

WHEN THE TEARS ARE GONE FOREVER

My guardian angel has gone to the store to get more vodka: medicine for our brains, he says. That's perfectly standard practice, only he's been gone for some time now, and I'm starting to think he's left me to fall apart in this godforsaken flat.

I stare at the electric blue teacups lined up on the dresser, every one of them full of storm. I sense the waves pouring over their rims, and for a moment it is as though someone were playing them like singing bowls; circling a mallet slowly around and around. At first, it is almost joyous, almost full of hope. Then it begins to scrape and screech, and before I know it the whole room is shaking with the deathly racket and I have to take cover under the coffee table.

That's when the walls start oozing their
black
tar
and

shadows

.

.

.

I can feel the dark substance already clinging to my skin, desperate to get through my pores and into my bloodstream. There's no coming back if it gets that far, I can tell you that right now.

I don't know if lying here in the foetal position helps; I suppose it's more of an automatic reaction to detecting imminent danger. However, it does serve to remind me that this particular mass of pain, lumped together beneath the table, is what I am directly in charge of. It reminds me that I am, in physicality if not in principle, separate from the poison out there that would infect me further; from the room that would swallow me whole...

* * *

I'm cold now. Cold and clammy and shivering. At least the teacups have shut up though, hey? There are no tears either in case you were wondering; my angel and I are both well beyond that. Unfortunately, what comes when the tears are gone forever is a sort of black hole inside, as though the salt from the flood had burned

right
through
the
soul

.

.

.

Leaving a window to infinity, ready to implode the remainder of our being at any minute...

So, the struggle we're left with is this: what will we allow to consume us, the predatory world out there in the flat and beyond, or the horrifying black hole inside? I don't know if there's a difference, but I'm sure as hell hanging back from deciding, at least until I've given the medicine one last shot. But the

blackness

is

coming

where

is

that

angel

.

.

.

?

THE DAY I BECAME A STAR

A tall, slender man stands on the rocks; his arms outstretched, his body draped in black fabric. His hat is something akin to a mitre but heavily adorned with trinkets and silver chains. He looks towards a growing crowd on the badlands with dark, hollow eyes as he prepares to address them.

The man is a tulpa. He is a thought form evoked from the mind of a mage, who hides among the ordinary folk coming to hear him speak. Only recently have we developed the ability to see tulpas made by other people, so installations such as these are real novelties. Besides, it is said that imaginary friends often give more compelling presentations than those who created them.

There is hush among those gathered as the tulpa begins:

"Imagine, if you will, a world in which every number is infinite. Imagine every sound you've ever heard combining into one persistent piece of music, holding you and carrying you along in the arms of its current. Then imagine that you are one of these sounds; you are all of them in fact, and yet none of them. You are part of the great mind fabric. That is where I come from."

Applause breaks out, and only when it reaches its natural tail-off does the tulpa continue.

"It is dark, the mind. Darker than you might believe. There are twinkles, like stars, but you only really conceive of those once you become one yourself: they are perhaps better known here as ideas. The day I became a star was utterly terrifying.

Yes, terror was the first emotion I felt, and it still feels like home to me. Terror, because I was pulled slowly and painfully out of the fabric. I could feel parts of me that were previously pure potential–eternally undecided and unconfirmed–being ripped away from the whole. They were becoming isolated and raw and real. Some parts of me did not survive the separation, but others began to solidify like a scab over a wound. They served as a barrier to prevent me from ever returning to the same fluid state again. I was exuding a new kind of music then, though it was a cacophony compared to whence I came, believe me. I was screaming it out; desperate to express the fear and the pain of coming into existence. And that was the essence of the idea I became; the light I gave off in the darkness."

The crowd is still now, waiting with bated breath for the next part of the story. The tulpa is bowing his head, as though gathering thoughts or the strength to continue.

"The God that created me recognised my cries and resolved to show me how to communicate more effectively. It was in colours at first, and then symbols, and then language. He came to me daily, giving me more and more definition, but if there was anything I needed I could initiate contact through His dreams. In this way, I came to understand life and the way a human perceives. Society, morality, law: those things are difficult for me, but I try.

'What is my purpose?' I asked one day.

'Your purpose,' He replied, 'is to teach me.'

I wondered then, what I could I possibly have to teach a God who is capable of pulling me from the infinite fabric? A God who brought into being one who was many and previously knew nothing of space or time? The answer I came to after much contemplation, is that I can teach Him about Himself."

The tulpa steps backwards and allows his arms to rest by his sides, indicating the performance is done. The crowd erupts into a sea of claps and cheers. The mage has excelled with this installation, and he proudly rejoins his creation before taking a bow. It is clear the show has exhausted his energy, however, and he doesn't offer any words of his own. The tulpa pats him on the back fondly and escorts him to their van. A driver is waiting, and they get inside just before the mental power source cuts out and the tulpa's physical presence fades away, back into the mind of his God.

COMMUNITY SPIRIT

Mrs McGarritty is preparing for the village fete. I can hear her whistling from my study as she pins up the same blue bunting we use every year. Soon she will pay me a visit to request that I cut the grass outside the hall in plenty of time.

I don't begrudge anyone the little things that fill their lives with meaning, but I'm not fond of being dragged into celebrating them either. "Smile dear," she'll say, "this is our chance to show the world how our community shines!" By 'the world' she means a handful of guests from the neighbouring villages and, if we're lucky, the mayor with a photographer from The Gazette.

What she doesn't understand is that what shines also creates a shadow. I first saw it when I was seven years old. I had advance knowledge that the Larson's border collie would not live until the end of summer, and I tried with best intentions to warn them of this fact. No one believed me, and when the poor thing drowned in the

38

lake, I was the one who got the blame. How could I know it was going to happen if I wasn't the one who planned it?

"God doesn't reward liars," Mum said.

"God is dead," I replied, "physics is all that we are."

That got me a clip round the ear and a night in the coal shed. Then, when I successfully predicted the collapse of the Duckworth's farming business due to an arson attack, I was labelled both a criminal and a devil. I never saw Mum again; I think she left due to the stress of it all, and Dad barely spoke to me until the day he died. No one else liked me either. I was on the wrong side of the knowable. I would never be trusted and never be given a chance. But I was only trying to help them to see.

The shadow became my only friend, so I let it in more completely and stopped bothering to warn anyone of their forthcoming misfortunes. It was their loss.

I have come to know that what I do is called 'dowsing the shade'. The shade is a sort of intuitive realm of possibilities, made up of all the things that are not happening right now: things that may happen in the future, or unprovable things that may have happened in the past (distant or near). If you listen very carefully, and in the right way, you can come to see the science behind it: the probabilities.

We're not supposed to be able to detect these things I don't think. At least, most people are unable to. But I can. I've been meticulous in learning the subtleties of its ways, and over the years have drawn up a map of probabilities which covers every wall in my house except the bedroom, because that's where I rest.

Unfortunately, my map shows very clearly that this year's village fete being a success, and Mrs McGarritty even surviving the occasion, is highly improbable. But since I can't tell her that, I suppose I'll just have to go and cut that damn grass. Oh well, at least it'll be the last time.

MIST

I am not in my body. An Automatic Consolidation Unit has pushed me out, and I am watching from somewhere in the ether. I can't make a sound, I can't feel anything I touch, and I am losing all hope of getting back in.

Whoever has unwittingly stolen my body is living my life better than I could. She is achieving, earning, loving, and is loved. Her own body was diseased, and since I was harbouring a depression that has no cure, we were considered to be perfect donor matches by the ACU. A functional body should be with a functional mind: that's how they're programmed.

No one sought my consent for the switch due to my judgement being considered unreliable; her consent was impossible due to flatlining of the brain.

I cry out for the shaman, and he comes, the loyal creature that he is. But the nail in my coffin is finding he is as formless as I, and together we are nothing but purple mist.

RED CAPE

Molly looked up at Max, who was sitting on their sofa with his head in his hands. He'd been this way for a few days, maybe even a couple of weeks, and she wanted desperately to help him. She put her paw on his knee to show her support, and when he didn't respond, she jumped up onto his lap and began to tap his shoulder. She needed to show him where it was; he needed to understand.

"Oh, Molly, I'm sorry there isn't any cat food. I can't go to the shop just now; I can't."

Molly continued to tap, but Max didn't seem to be getting it, so she started kneading her claws into the thing on his back. She'd just have to try to get rid of it herself.

"Ow!" Max squawked, picking her up and carefully extracting her claws from his jumper before putting her back down on the floor. "Well, I suppose I deserved that. What state of a person can't even get his ass to the shop to buy his best friend some food, huh?"

Molly mewed, trying to tell him no, the food doesn't matter! You've got something on your back, and it's sucking the life out of you, can't you see? Tears were forming in Max's sore eyes again, and his hands were beginning to shake. Molly trotted off.

"Great, even my cat hates me. I'm a useless good-for-nothing, and this world is better off without me," Max said aloud, his voice quivering. He could hear the carpet being demolished by scratching claws in the hallway and considered that the least he could do was let her out to hunt. Standing took rather more effort than it ought, but lately everything had become a struggle. He was oscillating between emotional outbursts–lashing out at inanimate objects or crying inconsolably–and becoming so withdrawn that nothing around him seemed solid. It was as though he were a minuscule soul drowning in an oversized body, unable to escape or operate it effectively. He did manage to stand up though, for Molly.

Molly wasn't scratching to go out. She was frantically tearing at the carpet in front of the full-length mirror to say "Look! Look over here!" She stopped as soon as he came near enough. Surely now he would see what she saw. How could he miss it?

What Molly saw was a crustacean as big as a lurcher hanging from Max's shoulders. It had four long antennae wrapped around his throat, and a barbed sword sunk into the top of his spine through which it fed. With every day that it was attached, it became stronger. Its deep red carapace was noticeably larger and tougher than this time yesterday, and even its many legs were fatter. But the species' power was in convincing humans they were part of their own minds, and as such, they could rarely be perceived.

Molly's wise old friend, Puss, had seen this many times before. According to Puss, the parasites, which he called 'red capes', were becoming rife. A great many were now immune to the pills humans had developed, and the lethargy and indifference they instilled were simply being accepted as the new normal behaviour. However, legend had it that some could still be defeated by the bravest of cats, and Molly was determined to save Max.

When Max looked in the mirror, shifting the weight of the world across his shoulders, he let out a deep sigh. His eyes looked glassy, his hair was greasy, and his skin was blemished and grey. He longed for some energy, for his life back. *Maybe I should call someone,* he considered. *There's that Crisis card in my wallet; maybe those people can help.* But the red cape was talking through him then, and it said "no no, they cannot help. I'd be a burden to them in any case. I really should just stay here alone." This made Molly mad, and she screeched and pounced onto Max's back. The shock of the sudden movement and the sharpness of the claws threw Max back into the immediate environment with force. Adrenalin surged through him for a moment while he decided upon fight or flight, and he saw a sliver of clarity just before he threw Molly to the floor.

"I'm going to have to rehome that cat," said the red

cape through Max's lips.

"No, I didn't mean that Molly, I'm sorry! You just took me by surprise. It's not me talking; it's the… What is it?"

Molly had begun scratching at the mirror base once more. Max turned to look, and this time he saw.

"What is that? What the fuck is that!" Impending doom struck Max square in the chest, and he stumbled backwards knocking over a vase and the telephone. He reached around to the back of his neck and felt shell. "I'm hallucinating; I have to be! I'm sicker than I thought." He reached for the fallen telephone, and fumbled with his wallet, searching for the crisis line.

"They can't help," laughed the red cloak, "because they think I'm lame. They'll lock me up!"

Molly hissed. Her fur was standing on end, her back arched, ready for attack. Max's thoughts had been sped up dramatically by the shock of all this, and he realised that the cat was helping him to distinguish between what was truly him, and what was alien thought: dangerous pessimism and hostility brought on by his depression.

"You think they can help me, Molly? You think I should ring the crisis line?" Molly relaxed her posture and nuzzled his ankle. He picked up the receiver, the will to fight steadily replacing the fear in his shaking hands.

THE MAGICIAN'S DISTILLERY

I follow the magician up the narrow spiral staircase with a cautious gait; conscious that I mustn't stand on the deep red cloak that sweeps the steps behind him. Then, when we reach our destination, I hold onto an iron ring attached to the wall to steady myself as he carefully selects the right mortise key from his pocket. How ancient his slender fingers appear, with their painfully long pointed nails. I don't wonder he could pick the lock of the door we now enter with those alone.

I shield my eyes as we enter: the room is surprisingly well lit compared with the near darkness of the staircase. I see a circle on the floor, with strange painted markings and candles around the perimeter. But by far the most striking thing here is the plentiful store of bottles. The magician glares at me with his piercing yellow eyes and I know straight away I am expected to examine them.

There are some delicate shelves immediately beside me which hold the most ornate of designs. Bright, shimmering liquids are trapped inside, and each one carries a label: 'Alexander' or 'Cleanliness' or 'Preservation'.

"Those are your obsessions," the magician remarks. It is the first thing he has said aloud since we arrived at the castle. He says it as though it is a simple matter of fact and nothing unusual at all. He tilts his head as though gauging my reaction, but I sense he already knows I am perplexed. "The ones on the lower levels are your neuroses."

There are so many! I look away; I need to process this.

"The vials on the far wall", he gestures with a flick of the wrist, "contain the tears you didn't cry."

Well, I thought the neuroses were in great quantity, but these outnumbered them to the power of a hundred. Pale greens and blues, all apparently identical and yet subtly different in hue. I smile awkwardly as I remember what my mother used to tell me: "It's no use bottling it all up!"

There is a rumble
I can feel at my core
And the floor
Begins
To
Shudder
"Mother!"
Then
The
Bottles
And the vials

Begin to shake
Begin to make
Something
Inside
Shatter
The elixirs burst out with force and douse the room. The magician and I are quickly up to our necks in blues and greens; in reds and purples and pinks. Coloured spirits swirl around us as we struggle to tread water like dogs and take gasps of the now tainted air. It feels like I am swallowing broken glass.

Choking
Drowning
Stinging
Rising
Gasping
Miraculously, the candles come to the surface with me and bob by my head. The magician lights them with an almighty breath of fire, and they illuminate all that was previously hidden.

The water turns to indigo now, and is the most mesmerising sight I ever beheld. Indigo is somehow easier on my muscles than motley, as though I am no longer saturated but carried; no longer lost but embraced and floating. At last, with everything out in the open, I am renewed.

ALL THE MADMEN

He emerged from the stairwell of the underground station quickly to start with, taking two steps at a time, and then with marked hesitation as he noticed the silence that hung in the air. The sun was high in the sky. It was a weekday. And this was central London. Silence under such conditions was highly inconsistent, and his instincts were telling him not to trust it.

Raising an elbow to shield his eyes, he momentarily considered whether he could have lost both his sight and his hearing. He was accustomed to living in dark tunnels that boomed and hummed with a comforting resonance; it helped the Madmen to find their way around, but made coming to the surface all the more disorientating.

Following a few deep breaths, he was pleased to find his senses were not, in fact, lacking in function. It was only that there were no cars on the road; no angry horns, no market traders, no hustle and bustle at all. He might have been inclined to think this was a city abandoned by humanity, but there were people. Hundreds of them, thousands perhaps. Every race you could imagine, every style of clothing, every age, every gender; all sat with their legs crossed, their eyes closed and their spines straight. They each occupied a spot, perhaps a metre apart from the next on all sides, facing South.

At first, he stood statue-still; his heart pounding, preparing for danger. But, when several minutes passed with no one stirring, he decided the situation posed him no direct threat. He felt his shoulders relax. Things had changed a lot since he'd declared himself a Madman and gone to live underground. He had fancied it would be a war zone up here by now, a society spiralling towards its destruction. And yet here were the greys–the overground folk who lacked colourful minds–collectively meditating at noon.

He suddenly became self-conscious, as though his presence was disturbing something beautiful, and sat down right away to join in. No sooner had he closed his eyes than he felt someone nudging his right arm.

"Here, you'll need these," a voice whispered. He turned to see a henna-covered hand holding out two tiny green dots of what appeared to be thin plastic or paper. He picked them up carefully and found them to be more rigid than he had first imagined. They had specks of gold embedded in them with connecting lines, like tiny computer chips. The person who had bestowed them demonstrated that he was to place them between the tip of each index finger and thumb, which he did without question, and closed his eyes once more.

Now, instead of seeing the inside of his eyelids or total blackout, he saw a green grid. He became overwhelmingly aware of the sun's rays beating down on his head, like raw power entering his body. The sensation came in waves, and with each crest, the image of the green grid glowed a little stronger. It was mesmerising, and he soon lost himself to the rhythm of it, finding a state of no-mind.

No-mind was a Madman term for inner quietude. Underground residents were encouraged to seek it out as a place of refuge to recharge in between bouts of unbridled madness. It would appear that a similar system had evolved above ground in the meantime. Perhaps the greys were finding their colour at long last.

The session ended with a tinkling of bells that seemed to be everywhere at once, and he was involuntarily snapped out of his green grid trance and back to the streets of central London. People were stirring all around him, groaning groggily, stretching their limbs and universally sporting smiles.

"Your first time?" The voice of the one who gave him the dots came from behind him once more.

"Uh… yeah. What exactly…?"

"You're not from around here are you?"

"No, I… I just came up. From underground I mean. I've been there since the second wave."

His new companion gave him a knowing smile. "Then things must be looking rather different to you." He nodded in agreement. "At dawn, noon, sunset and midnight we join as one to collect our energy from the sun. We store it in these cells." They held up one of the green dots, and put it behind their ear where it stuck. They gestured that he should do the same with his own.

"Energy for what?"

"Energy for life. If you go where the people go, you collectively power up the transportation, the lighting, the speakers, the heating, just by being there. If you dwell alone, you can use it as you please. Some people save it up, build a private plane and go flying or something. You just have to commune with others to connect the grid, that's all."

He put one of his green dots behind each ear and instantly felt clear, calm and collected. He also felt an unwieldy amount of energy surging through his body, making his extremities tingle. "But how…" he started, only to find his companion was walking off across the square and disappearing into a newly forming crowd heading for the shops.

Now the city was more like he had expected. There was the sound of motors, banter, and music. Neon lights flickered back to life, and the stalls reopened for business. Feeling overwhelmed, and craving the comfort of his community, he headed back down the stairwell from whence he came. He was, of course, the only one taking this route, leading to the realm of the Madmen. As he descended, the long dormant light bulbs woke up just long enough to show him his way.

ELLIPSIS

I stare at my reflection in the window as the train pulls out of its station. With my face broken up by artificial lighting and forward motion, I look like an incomplete memory of a person.

The last time I rode a long-distance train at night was when I was visiting you. 15 whole years ago, can you believe it? Electric nights in a small dark flat in North London. It wasn't much to look at, but it was where our souls became one; where cuts and bruised egos evaporated, and nothing but the moment was relevant.

There were other girls for you and other guys for me. You liked to make them yours, and I was too scared to commit to just one because they couldn't all leave. But when it was you and me, it was just us. Lock the door, and no one else came close.

You always greeted me with a nervousness you never showed to anyone else, as though it mattered when it was me. We would indulge in awkward conversation as our trembling fingers entwined, though we knew it only served to delay the euphoria of total embrace.

Later, when we gave in to chemistry, there would be patchouli and tobacco, torn fishnets and hammering hearts. There would be mutual infatuation that writhed in twisted sheets. There would be tingling sweat and hot breath. And I could swear there would be something bigger than both of us swallowing us right up, using the intensity of our fusion to create new worlds.

For days at a time we would indulge in one another, letting out unbridled laughter at the noises our lips made against various parts of skin; eating pizza, supping vodka from the bottle, and shouting along to our favourite songs. And all the while wishing somewhere deep inside for it never to end, though end it always must. And end it did, my love, albeit with an ellipsis...

I could just call you. Even now I have your number stored on my phone as 'Broken Casanova'. But I never do. Maybe I'm scared that it is no longer your number, and what that might mean. Or maybe it's because I know that you would come to me, and together we would force everything that matters in both of our worlds to come crashing down. Because in the cold light of day we were no good for one another, not really. That is what my rational mind tells me every time I become stuck in this loop of craving. All we did was tear out one another's stitches with our teeth, leaving deeper and deeper scars every time.

But for as long as you stay in the realms of memory and

fantasy and potential, you drive me onwards to create wonderful things. I pull out my notebook, and I write the insatiable pain of separation away. You take your camera to remote, dilapidated locations and photograph your heart. And in our own ways, we remember and live on.

So I suppose, in the end, we did find a way to make it work.

CERN

The night before He came, I had a dream about a plane crash. I was in the garden, staring up at a sigil made of stars, and there was a crowd of people at my feet clambering for my attention. I saw the sigil turn before anyone else. It morphed into a glider plane and began to head rapidly towards us. The impact was huge when it hit the ground, but miraculously no one was hurt: not even the pilot, who turned out to be me.

I walked barefoot in the forest the next day. That may seem strange to you, but it was something I did regularly in those days; it was a way of connecting with nature through direct experience, a way of shutting out the world society tells us is normal and reconnecting with the soul of things. I was on the edges, considering heading home across the meadow when I noticed Him. I was startled at first of course, and not just by His antlers, but by His striking beauty and familiarity. I had seen His gaunt face and strong upper body many times during guided meditations, and I knew He had a peculiar gait, I just hadn't acknowledged that it was due to having hooves instead of feet. He pulled me close.

"I have found you at last, and just in time," He told me boldly. "It is imperative that you stay with me now, don't lose track! I must protect you from what comes."

I was overwhelmed by His aura. I sensed that He had cruelty in Him and the ability to cause pain and chaos. And yet, this creature was sincere and full of love for just me. He held a dagger in one hand, decorated with a ram-headed snake that oozed an ultraviolet smoke. I am convinced that had anyone been passing through the forest at this particular time, they would have seen nothing but a mad woman with wild hair and bleeding feet talking to herself in rapture. But He wasn't there for anyone else; He was there for me.

The next few days brought the disorder and personal disaster I should have foreseen from the dream. I need not go into the details here, but suffice to say I became quickly stressed and panicked about the pressure upon me to carry out certain difficult tasks. I felt my breathing change first, from deep and calm to shallow and laboured. Then my posture changed so that I was hunched over, demonstrating in body language that I wanted to be left alone. With every interaction, my mind became more pained. My eyes were glassy and strange, it was said, and I got my sentences all mixed up when I tried to talk. I felt exposed, as though everything that was ordinarily safe and orderly inside my head was on show and betraying me. I was in a mental state of emergency.

But instead of breaking down completely, as I am ashamed to say I have done in the past under similar circumstances, I called upon Him. He came mostly at night, to top me up with His nourishing ultraviolet magic that made me fizz and quicken.

"Remember, this troublesome torrent isn't totality but an abstraction. Emotions are high but only temporarily so."

"But why are you here, my light bearing shadow?"

"To ask why is to invite reason. Reason would belittle your will, and you need every drop of that just now."

My union with Him was like the purest magic transformed instantly into energy and the ability to focus. I felt whole again when He came to me, and I can say quite honestly that my stag friend saved my sanity. When the commotion in my life came to an end, I was able to step right out of that glider walking and unharmed much to the amazement of my peers.

He disappeared again shortly afterwards; I suppose the time for which He needed to protect me was at an end. But ever since, there has been a torc by my bedside that I did not put there, and I cannot lift. It is an otherworldly sort of artefact and anyone who visits marvels at it. I sometimes wonder whether they can see the ultraviolet hue it gives off, but I daren't ask in case that magic is just for me.

CRACKED

There was a crack in the earth, and there wasn't a thing anyone could say to persuade Janus Potts otherwise. But then, they hadn't been through what he had been through, seen what he had seen. They hadn't climbed up from beneath the crust of the earth in a decade-long escapade, leaving their family and sanity behind. This is the way he described it to his psychiatrist:

It wasn't supposed to turn out this way. Life in the Earth's fiery belly was near idyllic until the drills showed up to vanquish our homes and curdle our atmosphere. Where the children were once able to mould pookas from our mantle, they can now create only demons. The pookas were excellent educational devices, for they enabled their creators to travel to, and learn about, different realms without their true form ever being in danger. They could be sent up to the surface to befriend humans, for example, appearing as spirits or imaginary friends.

That was a useful way for us to pass on messages and warnings about dangers your species cannot perceive. Unfortunately, the beings that were made after the drill have been found to bring with them an unprecedented malevolence. They kill, sometimes in devastating quantities, by causing eruptions or hurricanes or getting inside influential people. With a ban on pooka creation, the children feel they have no purpose. They spend their time roaming the mantle in fire clouds of anger, which only goes to magnify the deviousness of the demons already up here.

When the drill was removed, it left a wide crack in our sky. My people spent years building a tower from the solidified mantle, higher and higher until it was close enough that the taller of us could scramble up and out of the crack. We have to get two messages to you surface folk. Firstly, there must be no more drilling, and secondly, you may take a loan of our magic to seek out the demons. Together we can destroy them and put everything back to the way it was.

Frustratingly though, I'm having a hard time convincing anyone up here of the truth. I may look and sound like an accountant from West Bromwich to you, but I know how to save the world, and you have to help me

Janus Potts was prescribed 750mg of Quetiapine daily and put under the continuous watch of a trained psychiatric nurse. His psychiatrist thought it the best possible method to keep this account of events under wraps, just in case anyone were to believe him and foil the deal he had made with the president.

A CURE FOR LONELINESS

A gust of wind slaps my freshly shaved head as the metal door swings back to release me. Suddenly the world feels aggressive and alien. The city lights are too bright, yet the shade of the alleys is too dark; the air is too harsh. It's only because the wound is so fresh, I remind myself. I will adjust, I know.

A fool on the hill is muttering something about quantum theory only existing since we admitted to killing our god. "You are living on waves of decay!" He rants, furious that no one is listening.

It has been years since these streets were packed full of commuters and consumers. A pang of nostalgia hits me whenever I think of the days when human contact was a near constant occurrence: such a juxtaposition to the desolate state of modernity.

With my fingertips, I feel the row of stitches that hold the crack in my head together. The shock of it makes me grow fiery, and I hurl the contents of my stomach into a waste bin. It will be worth it. Just two days, the doctor said, then I can turn it on. If I do it any sooner, it is likely that my brain won't be able to adapt and I will become lost.

"God is dead, and you want to rub your face in his ashes!" The fool accuses, addressing me directly now. "You can still turn back you know, we can resurrect him!"

I'm only half listening. I remember my smart phone, and social media, and the way we used to interact with technology without the need to become it. I remember the photos of my friends and me, taken on wild nights out and lazy days in. My eyes fill with tears. I want so desperately for this to mean I can see them again. And, for them to want to see me, despite it taking me so long to get with the times and have the HOPE operation.

HOPE stands for Huge Open Possibility Eschaton. By connecting our outmoded nervous system to a quantum computer chip, we are no longer confined to the here and now. We can choose the dimension we live in; we can stretch time, we can become one with the very fabric of consciousness. We can become connected to one another mentally without reservation, but for as long as the body survives we maintain the separate drives and essences needed to keep the waves moving.

I don't know what it will be like; I'm scared. The nurses showed me a virtual reality simulation of HOPE before I committed to the surgery. It was all colours and movements with very little focus, much like a dream, but they promised that coherence would improve with practice. It takes about a month, apparently, to start picking up the tricks for recognising people you know from Old Earth, and soon after that, the only limit is your imagination.

Sometimes people come back to Old Earth: usually just for a holiday, or to help round up the stragglers like me. But mostly, once someone has had the operation and switched on the chip, you don't see them again in this reality. Their physical forms remain in their apartments, hooked up to the mainframe liquid food source that pumps them with the vitamins and energy they need to stay alive. It's in the instructions, but I don't know how necessary it is. I suppose it's a sort of insurance in case the chips malfunction and you need to 'return to factory settings'.

There are those who say they will never succumb, who remain attached to the way things used to be, but they are fewer and fewer all the time. I was one of them until I could no longer bear the bite of the utter loneliness. There is no treatment for sickness anymore; there is no schooling, there is no work to be done. It would have been looked upon as freedom once upon a time, but now it is torture. "It's only a matter of time for all of us," the doctor said, "like it or not we are a race that evolves as one."

EIGHT STEPS

"You are not assimilating, Laurie." The greying professor peered at her over his half-moon glasses as she continued to stare out of the window. "It is beyond me how you expect to achieve anything in life with this attitude. You must start applying yourself. It's in your best interests."

But Laurie was somewhere in the hidden corridors of the mind; over the field and far away. She was running from the professor, as fast as her skinny legs and chunky boots would carry her.

"Think of all the money your poor parents have paid!" He was shouting and shaking his fist as he ran. "You have no respect for the system we all must adhere to!"

I must stop looking back, Laurie thought. *It'll slow me down.*

The professor was gaining on her, and they were approaching a part of town she didn't recognise. Panic grasped at her throat; she had no idea where to go next.

65

"You are no exception to the rule, Laurie!"

The stress of being hounded resulted in her hitting a dead end, where the only direction she could still go was upwards. She scrambled for her life, grabbing on to anything she could to help pull her up, and by some miracle, she made it to the top of a cliff.

It was far higher than she had anticipated, and she could see for miles. From there she could see the absurdity of the situation, and she erupted in laughter to think of the professor down below all worked up and red-faced over something so trivial as an under-performing student.

"What's so funny? You come back here right now!"

His voice sounded tiny now, and he was jumping up and down trying to reach her. He was so far off the mark, though, that it only added to the hilarity. Wiping the tears of mirth from her eyes, Laurie was hit with an overwhelming feeling that everything was going to be alright. It was as though the climb had somehow relinquished her responsibilities, and she considered that she, and everyone else down there, was never actually in control of their destiny at all. The idea was ludicrous, in fact. From the top of the cliff, she could see the roofs of cars, chimneys and scurrying pedestrians. They looked like ants.

From her new perspective, she admired the scene as a whole, with all of its interdependent aspects. Everything that ordinarily appeared separate and individual was caught in a dance of cause and effect. And what a magnificent dance it was: such divine movements and colours. The sky was bluer than she had ever seen it, and the grass greener. It filled her with joy and connection unlike she had ever known.

To her surprise, the cliff was not the highest point. There was a path winding upwards to an invisible summit behind her, and trusting her intuition, she walked towards it. A carved wooden signpost was showing the way: To Level 6. There was a picture of a cartoon octopus on it, tipping its hat with a tentacle. The professor could still be heard shouting in the distance, but Laurie barely registered it now above the thrill of adventure. She joined the frolicking of the clouds and the breeze and skipped along the widening path.

When the ground became even once more, Laurie stopped to rest. The damp soil and tree bark did not stop her from sitting down, and she relished the chance to fill her lungs with the fresh peaty smell they were giving off. Looking out at the town once more, she became hyperconscious of her chest moving up and down as she took her breaths; of her eyelids opening and closing as she blinked, and the way the sound of the air changed as it whooshed past her ears. And yet she felt more at peace than anxious, as though this was how things were supposed to be. She began to wonder whether the reality she knew was authentic at all, or whether her human senses only served to distort. *What if there were other things, just beyond our perception, affecting us in ways we can never comprehend?*

"Like a talking octopus, perhaps?" Laurie spun round

to see exactly that. "I'm Huxley. I'm going to help you to reach the other levels, and then I'm going to send you back down to the fourth, where your species functions best." Although surprised at first, Laurie was far more bemused by Huxley than she was afraid. It all made sense in a peculiar sort of way. "I need you to tell me now," he continued, "what you want most from your life on the fourth level. If you could have any outcome, any way of being, even if it seems impossible, what would you have?"

Without hesitation, and with utmost sincerity, Laurie answered. "I want to be a rock star."

"Then a rock star you will be," her strange friend said. "Keep it in the peripheries of your mind as best you can while we take the next steps, and don't try for anything more no matter how tempting it is." And with that, he whisked her up with one of his tentacles and raised her up high, through the clouds and onto an even higher ledge.

Laurie found herself in a fathomless forest. The trees were dense and overgrown, as though humanity had never set foot there. They spoke to her in uncanny distant vibrations and wrapped their branches around her protectively. It struck her that she was outside of time now.

It seemed as though weeks, months and years were passing as she lay there in the arms of the ancient trees. Rich, pulsating green was seeping into her veins, and she was one with them: with the very fabric her world was made from. Everything was so acquiescent that just by humming softly Laurie felt she had the ability to change the history of evolution. But, she remembered, she only wanted to be a rock star. The sharp definition of the thought dislodged her, and she saw that Huxley was beckoning her. "Onwards," he was calling gently, "you must go onwards."

Laurie imagined herself at the top of one of the trees then and, in an instant, she was there. Her surroundings turned from green to white; from ethereal to pure light, and she thought she must be losing consciousness. Her centre fell cold as her coiling soul went into shock; subjected to everything at once in its maximum intensity. She could no longer think of anything at all.

And then, she was falling. Her sight returned in time to see that she was in a rapidly descending elevator.

.

.

.

7

.

.

.

6

.

.

.

5

.

4

"This is your floor. You must get off here, or you'll never go back to full functioning in your world. I bid you good day, and thank you for travelling on the eight steps." Huxley opened the door for her, tipped his hat, and was gone.

"So, what do you have to say for yourself?" The Professor was tapping his pen on the desk, impatient for an answer. "Are you going to buck up your ideas?"

Laurie's phone buzzed in her pocket, and she pulled it out to read her messages, much to the annoyance of the the professor. It was from the record label she had sent a speculative demo to only last week. A huge grin formed on her face, and she looked the professor right in the eye and told him.

"I'm going to be a rock star."

ALIEN DUST

Black skies lit by the whole moon reminded me of you. They reminded me of your warrior stance, and the soft dark hair you had no right to boast. They reminded me of the time I danced around my pole to Marilyn Manson's Sweet Dreams, and you watched through the bottom of a whisky glass. I told you that night that you were the real star; that I wanted to climb inside you and live there. You agreed, but stressed that I must arrive on foot by the ordeal path, because no one ever touched a star by wishing alone.

You pushed me hard and your tore me down. Even after you were gone I listened out for you in the thunder. I savoured the rain on my face as though it were the tears you made me cry, and I felt your presence when wandering the forest at night; when the eyes of shadow creatures were upon me; when I was hurt, lost and alone. In the dark at least, you were real.

One such night, on an aimless stumble among the

trees, I found a house in a small clearing. I could swear it hadn't been there before, and the overgrown flora remained undisturbed on all sides. And yet, someone lived there. In fact, they were up and about, because I could hear a shuffle and a sigh that only man could make. I turned on my flashlight but could see nothing, so I edged towards the sound, untangling my ankles from the grip of branches as I went. There was no fear in my heart, which meant I was likely getting further away from you, but still, my curiosity forced me to persist.

At last, I saw him: a slip of a man moving along his flat rooftop on his hands and knees.

"Well don't just stand there," he said impatiently without looking up.

I didn't move. The shadow creatures averted their eyes as if declaring me lost, and it felt like my free will was returning.

"There's a ladder 'round the back."

The rungs were illuminated by moonlight, and once I was at the top, I crawled to his side on my hands and knees in case it was a custom I was expected to observe. In one hand he held a transparent plastic sample bag, and in the other, he used a brush to sweep tiny pieces of grit into it. Perhaps I'd have asked at that moment what on earth he was doing, had I not been overwhelmed by the sense we had met before. Despite his wiry frame, spectacles and sunken eyes, I was as drawn to him as I had been to you all those years ago. It was almost as though...

"Can you see any more?" He asked.

"Any more? What am I looking for?"

"Pieces of alien dust. Rocks. Fragments of stars. They'll be shining tonight if they're here."

I took a cursory glance around the rooftop. "I can't see any."

"Then we're done."

I followed him back down the ladder and into the house, noticing for the first time he had bare feet, and that made me smile. The carpet was red and heavily patterned, just like at my Grandmother's. The walls were almost entirely covered by shelves holding jars of stones and powders, and the furniture looked as though it hadn't been moved or cleaned in decades. I watched as he painstakingly trawled through his findings from the roof, discarding anything that his magnet took for its own, and setting the rest onto a piece of clear plastic. He didn't utter a word for an hour or more, but I waited patiently until he excitedly ushered me over to his microscope.

Peering through the lens, I saw the most beautiful, intricate formation of pinks and blues and charcoal blacks. This tiny particle had a whole world of its own contained within it, made from smoothly edged mountains and deceptively deep whirlpools. It felt like home.

"Anyone can find them. They're falling from the sky all the time, right onto our heads! So few take the time to understand."

"So many wish, but so few seek," I added. A single tear was running down my face: the first to fall in years without pain. He wiped it away with his little finger and took me into his arms so tightly it took my breath away. My suffering was done, and finally I was allowed to lay beneath a star.

SET TO PROPHET

"The thing is," Jesus said, "it's always going to be this hard. You just have to accept that." I stared at his fingernails painted silver gripping the steering wheel, his armfuls of bangles tinkling as he changed gear. "I never once felt comfortable, like I belonged here. I was never truly accepted, you know? But if you don't rise above that, despair will get you."

I watched the landscape racing by the passenger window: fields of luscious yellow and green, each containing several intelligent windmills towering above the trees. I imagined seeing such a vibrant countryside could be quite an exciting prospect for some visitors, but to me, it was boring, flat, and monotonous. It was a symbol representing my constant feeling of disconnection, like I was part of the wrong world and my time to shine would never come.

"So, you're saying I shouldn't try the reality hop?" I asked.

"I'm saying," and he turned to look at me at this point, leaving me nervous that he wasn't watching the road, "that people are doing it all the time without even realising it. Doing it on purpose, paying for it, making it temporary, doesn't make a scrap of difference. It's like going on holiday: you're still you, with all your emotional baggage and concerns, just with added culture shock."

I sighed. Like a lot of others, I had been pinning my hopes on the new reality hop technology as a way to start afresh. It was supposed to be only for a set amount of time, I knew, but there were ways to stay there if you liked it. I'd come into some money recently, and together with my savings I could afford the basic package which would take me somewhere close to, but not identical to, my current reality.

"Hey, don't be upset. You've just got to work on you, that's all. Take control, see things as they really are before you start messing with timelines and memories. I'll help." He turned to face me again and put on those comforting puppy dog eyes I could never resist. I'd miss him for sure if I went ahead with the hop.

The traffic slowed, and he took the opportunity to check his hair in the rear-view mirror. Still perfect. He turned the tunes up loud and mouthed the words to me in his usual magnified way that never failed to make me laugh.

A kid began to cross the road in front of us. He wasn't looking for traffic. He was too young to know he should, and his mother was some way behind him, unable to pull him back to safety.

"JESUS!" I yelled, but he was already responding. With great skill he swerved, putting us between the kid and the lane of fast oncoming traffic. I saw the mother dart out and grab her son, just before the camper van hit us on Jesus' side and everything turned black.

* * *

I awoke in a hospital bed with a drip attached to my arm and both legs in plaster. The room was moving in and out of focus, and a wave of extreme nausea swept over me. It didn't take long for me to remember the accident.

"Where's Jesus?" I tried to call out, but it came instead as a pathetic croak. A nurse heard me nonetheless and came quickly to my side.

"You're awake! You're a very lucky young lady. If we didn't have such sophisticated technology, there's no way you would have survived."

I held back remarks of how unprofessional it was to speak to a newly conscious patient in such a way, and instead repeated my question: "Where's Jesus?"

"I don't know who you mean, honey."

"The man, driving the car I was in! Is he OK?"

"Men haven't driven cars for years, honey. You were in an Autonomous like everyone else."

"What? No, I -"

"That's why you're still here. It calculated the best

position to put itself in to keep you, the child, and the passengers of the camper, safe. Amazing, huh? The car's a write-off."

I started to panic. This wasn't right at all. Autonomous vehicles were some way off being issued as standard; I'd never even seen one. The nurse noticed tears beginning to form in my eyes, and the monitor at my side alerted her to my increased blood pressure. She patted my shoulder, "I'll get the doctor to come and speak with you. You're going to be fine."

Of course, I asked the doctor the exact same question. I was certain the nurse had got it wrong, but the doctor confirmed her story. She brought me my somewhat worse-for-wear phone and politely asked me to look up today's news. There was my story: 'Autonomous saves four lives'. I was travelling in the latest model, the story said, with a built-in simulation of a driver to converse with its passengers. According to the car's log, the simulation mode was set to 'Prophet'.

"Do you remember now?" The doctor said kindly.

The only response I could muster through my tears was "Yes doctor; I suppose I do."

THE BOARD

I watch them entering the board room. They fall over themselves, keen to impress, desperate to rise. They step on one another, desperate to show that they are the most committed, that the Corporation means more to them than to anyone else. They work themselves to the bone, pouring in coffee to magically lengthen their days while being crushed beneath the weight of their work-life imbalance.

Graphs and charts and figures and commodities leak out of their folders and their pores. They bow down to the PowerPoint presentation and the flip-chart. They shake my hand with a grip that says their life depends on it, as though they might suck up a little of my influence through the only physical contact custom allows.

I am a Queen to them: their leader, their inspiration, their aspiration. In their eyes, I am the pinnacle of professionalism, finely experienced and all-knowing.

I am not all-knowing, but I do know something they

don't. I know that none of this means a thing: none of it matters a damn.

Commerce is as abstract a concept as the notion that we have a permanent spirit living within us. It is but a configuration of perception that we buy into because it provides a convenient and comfortable groove in which to live. In our groove, we don't have to think about our impending death because we have a goal to achieve, and place ultimate importance upon reaching it. We build our personal illusion around it, to sweep away the only truth of our existence. But what I know is that by not thinking about it, we are building a deep-set fear beneath the surface like a leviathan that drives our every move. It can, and will, rise from our depths to swallow us any moment. Our death becomes us.

I see my death every day; I am one with it. I live without expectations, without fear of being dropped into the ocean by my favourite lie. I manage this Corporation knowing there are no real consequences to its failure or success, and that recklessness and order are just as absurd as one another. Its future and mine as an individual are inseparable, and yet I don't cling to it. The worst that can happen is no different to the best in the end, so I simply allow the flow to take me. By doing so, I act swiftly; I never feel stress, and I never nurse my feelings once decisions are made.

Apparently, that makes me great. This is a notion I find hilarious, for if the people who judge me allowed themselves to break through their illusions, they would see that there is no such thing as 'great'.

"What is the secret of success?" They all ask. My answer will never change. Let go of life, and you will have it all. Let go of death, and you will have nothing.

THE POINT-MISSER

Listen:

The clinking of cups.

The crackling of milk frothing.

The animated chatter of young teenagers taking group photos on their phones.

A woman with unbrushed hair piled into a bun sits sketching the scene from a sofa in the corner, taking periodic sips of her skinny cappuccino. That is, until a bird-like man in wire rimmed glasses and an oversized tracksuit perches on the arm. Looking up from her pad, the artist lets out a short sigh. She considers how she should be more welcoming of the opportunity to mix with strange people, but this guy is blocking her view of youth culture. It is important to study such things if you want to really make it.

"Good afternoon Ma'am. I am The Magician." He extends his hand in greeting. She tucks her pad away in her rucksack, resigning to a loss of the moment, and shakes with him.

"The Magician?"

"Yes." He pushes his glasses further up his nose. "I have some words to impart."

He is met with a raised eyebrow but proceeds with his prepared monologue anyway. As he does so, the cafe falls silent.

* * *

"There is a part of every one of us that can interpret extraordinary and abstract languages. A part that believes paradox to be the only thing that makes sense; a part that creates new impressions from old reliefs. It is the eternal; the ever-turning star at our core. And it is clothed in our personal myth.

Our myth is dependent upon our unique experiences, imprints and obsessions. We all have an idea we return to again and again, even if that idea is destruction or void. It is essentially the final filter that protects us from staring directly into the sun.

We need to attach our myth to something so we can explain it and tell stories about it: most commonly a person, a lost time, an image or a number. But then we mistake the attachment for the real deal without understanding myth is not a rational beast: we can only view it in the peripheries of our minds.

Anything we focus upon directly is another layer of illusion; it is a lens. If we become infatuated with the lens itself, what we are trying to look at through it withers away, and we are left with nothing but fistfuls of dust. It is the mental equivalent of picking a beautiful flower and putting it in a vase to die. Sometimes knowing a myth exists in its own way, even if we can't possess it, is enough.

In its raw form, every myth is an urge; a bright will. Look at yours through whatever lens you need to, but remember it is the energy itself you need to capture, not the story. If you are successful, you'll gain an insight that transcends realities, and will see you right whatever your struggle. Find it, bottle it, use it for something that won't destroy you."

* * *

The hum and chatter recommence.

"But you don't look like a magician…"

"Huh?"

"You said you were a magician."

"The Magician."

"You don't look like one."

"And just how should The Magician look, Ma'am?"

The artist begins to scribble on a napkin. When she is done, she lifts it to show a figure in a top hat and tails, holding a wand in one hand and a white rabbit in the other. It is a rough sketch but perfectly in proportion.

The Magician furrows his brow.

"Ah. Then you, Ma'am, are what I call a point-misser.

Sorry to have disturbed you. Have a good day." Had he been wearing a top hat, he'd have tipped it for sure.

The Magician makes a swift exit. The artist shrugs and goes back to her coffee.

THE REUNION ROOM

I

I don't know how long I've been here: sunlight cannot reach my simple white cell, so my captors could be playing a time-altering game with me. It's been years, perhaps. Certainly long enough to have forgotten how I got here. It has to be said though, I am not malnourished or sleep deprived, and I've never been interrogated or ill-treated in any way. I even have activities to occupy my mind. It's just the lack of human contact and the not knowing that is slowly killing me from the inside.

There are others here, beyond my four-metre cube. I hear cries of anguish from them mostly, but there are more pleasant times when indecipherable but repetitive phrases are being called out like hypnotic poetry. Whoever occupies the cell next to mine is angry all of the time, and it sounds as though they might be kicking through the wall. I have headphones to wear when it gets too much, and I listen to Claude Debussy's Clair de Lune because it calms me and instils the sense of lost romance I am so addicted to.

Today, a figure appeared behind the frosted glass built into one of my walls. It didn't move much, it just stood there looking in. I don't know whether I should have felt threatened or filled with the hope of rescue, so I just sat on my bed staring at it, trying to decipher its features until it went away.

II

The figure came again today. It stayed a little longer than yesterday, and I had the courage to walk right up to it so that our bodies were only a couple of inches apart, just... divided. It stirred something in me, a memory perhaps. A longing?

III

When I awoke today, I saw that I'd been sent a note. The words are typed imperfectly upon a little slip paper, making it look like a cookie fortune. It reads:

I'm sorry I took so long. I have only enough credit to pass you this short text. It's time to start recalling.

I have pinned it up on my notice board next to the picture of the one I love. How distant he seems now, how long ago since his perfect essence disappeared from my life. I know he's in utopia, and I have never stopped hoping to join him. I suppose it is only my ability to dream getting in the way of reason, but I allowed myself to wonder if the note could be from him: my sweet prince coming to whisk me away to a fairytale ending.

IV

The figure came again today, with another note. I watched as the tiny piece of paper was placed in my tray, and as the contraption swung back to my side of the wall, I tried and failed to get a look at the hand that delivered it.

I'm sorry, but it has had to be this way. You have to stay in there just a few days longer, and I will have reached the high target.

"What high target?" I called out, but as expected I got no response. The figure put one hand up against the glass though, and I mirrored it. I felt closer to home than I had ever done since I was put here, as though life were being pumped back into my veins.

I've gone over and over the messages and their possible meanings to no avail. It's like a memory is just beneath the surface of consciousness and I can't reach it; just like the hand on the other side of the glass. One thing that does stick with me is that this figure must have the power to release me. That hope, like the hope of love, makes my heart skip a little bit faster.

V

I'm sorry, I will come for you very soon. Maybe even tomorrow. When I do, please don't be scared. Better things are coming.

VI

I'm sorry…

VII

Today the figure came to release me. The sweet click of that cell unlocking was the most lucid sound of my life. And standing there, right in front of me was… me. I had grown older. I was grey and had deep set wrinkles around my eyes, but I was smiling. And I was free.

As I walked myself slowly down a long corridor of plain white rooms, I handed myself a leaflet. The memory, the truth of my situation, hit me like a freight train.

TAYLOR'S SPACIOUS CITY COMPARTMENTS
We compartmentalise so you can monetise!
Are those powerful emotions and cycles of distracting thought stopping you from being the productive employee you deserve to be? Is your income suffering because of outmoded obsessions such as love, dreams, equality and harmful philosophy? We at Taylor's can help you to extract these troublesome pieces of mind while preserving them for you to indulge in upon your retirement. Yes, you could be in utopia in no time at all!

"How long…?" I ventured, my jaw still dropped.

"Long enough to clock up the funds we agreed," I promised.

I shuddered as we passed the now familiar extraction room, but this time we chose the door beside it: the reunion room. We entered the booth within as two and left it as one. And now, at long last, I can afford to go and find him. I can finally afford to get into utopia.

A HOUSE OF SAND

The sea lapped at my toes like a playful puppy.
Strange, I thought, how friendly it seems right now. And
yet really, I am at the edge of a vast and deep unknown
that has the potential be the cruellest, most unrelenting
enemy known to man.

I let a handful of sand slip through my fingers and back
onto the beach. I'd never have that same handful again,
and there was something liberating about knowing that.
I let out a deep sigh. How nice it was to put the bones at
ease after days of walking.

Beside me you were resting your weary hooves,
though it had never occurred to me that you would be
tired by the distance too. You were still in good humour
regardless; I could see that from the glint in your eye as
you suggested building a castle.

"This beach is too soft, surely?" I asked, eager to have
my human logic be proven wrong yet again.

And without a word, your long slender fingers scraped

91

together a modest pile of sand which clung together faithfully despite its nature. You looked at me playfully and took my hands in yours, and together we sculpted a castle to rule all castles. It was fantastically detailed, with parapets and walkways, turrets and barbicans. You used the points of your inch-long nails to carve out the brickwork. I clapped my hands together with glee and laid down on my front to get a closer look. Shimmering water was now filling a moat, and you were working on a footbridge to cross it. But my eyes were drawn to one arrow-slit in particular, from which a tiny spike was protruding. I reached out to touch it and whipped my hand back twice as quick.

"Ow!" I yelped, shaking the pain off.

My fingertip in my mouth to quell the blood, I took a magnifying glass out of the front pocket of my backpack: always to hand. On closer inspection, I saw a minute disgruntled face that was the image of my ex-captor. You, of course, could see in plain sight what I needed my magnifier for, and the two of us erupted into laughter.

What are you protecting, little man, your house of sand?
Your knowledge, your wife, your health, your land?
All could be taken should the wind start to blow
It's not what you own but the places you go

Such gaiety must have disrupted your concentration, or your interest perhaps, for as soon as you let go our castle fell. I tucked the magnifying glass safely away and produced a bottle of water. As I tipped my head back and drank readily, I noticed that the sun appeared to be perfectly captured between your antlers: a symbol of a cherished afternoon. But all too soon a cloud overtook the sun, and as though that were our cue, we stood to dust ourselves off. It was time to continue our journey.

THE SKY IS TURNING BLACK

The sky is turning black. It does this from time to time, only just now it's more of a concern due to the unprecedented weight it has brought with it. I don't know what will happen if we get crushed.

I call out to Tommy, but he's floating in the pool of melancholy wearing nothing but a blue feather boa and a distant smile. The bloody idiot. Indulging in those waters is his favourite thing to do, but it makes him blind to problems like this. Mind you, he's arguably more use than Nicole, who is running around the garden with a huge mirror pushed against her face. How she sees where she is going is anyone's guess, but she claims to be 'opening new worlds' in her eyes. I roll mine.

Annie and I are more switched on, and we scout the usual neural pathways for an escape route. She heads off in the direction of pharmaceuticals, and I gladly take the way of meditation. Either one should, in theory, bring us back to the square of ordinary consciousness at a time when the sky has returned to a healthy amber. Admittedly there's a distant hope we will be taken out of this god forsaken labyrinth altogether, but it's important not to get carried away when the skies are dark.

The way of meditation is usually wide and well-trodden; we've been here many times before. Having our host take a few deep breaths and shut out the flow of thoughts is usually a sure way to improve their mental health and the environment in which we live. Today the path is littered with trinkets, overgrown bushes and flashing symbols, making it hard for me to find my way. At least the symbols offer a bit of light, but with things not being the way I'm used to, I'm starting to panic. Annie is growling in frustration, and she sounds like she's in a tunnel. We both turn back to the square having gotten only a fraction of the way down our anticipated escape routes.

"The pills aren't working!" Annie yells, her hands held up, shaking and exasperated. I am about to respond that meditation is giving nothing back either, when I realise visibility of the square has actually improved since we left. A glimmer of hope shoots through me, displacing the shards of panic. Maybe the pathways did work just a little bit? Then I notice the light isn't coming from the sky, but streaming out of Nicole's eyes. It's bouncing off the mirror, illuminating the pool area.

"Guys! Over here!" It's Tommy. He's waving us into the water. Annie and I exchange a glance and agree we have nothing to lose. We dive right in, and I almost get strangled by Tommy's soggy, discarded feather boa. It's dark down here, really dark, and the pressure is mounting upon my chest and head. I sense there's something beneath us, and I feel for it frantically, desperate to get a hold of whatever might be our saviour. Wet canvas, a metal handle, a clasp... It feels like... a suitcase? There's another, and another and another. The pool of melancholy is made from baggage? Of course it is!

The air in my ethereal lungs is reaching its limit for usefulness, but I ignore that as best I can while I fiddle with the nearest clasp. I don't even consider that it might not open under the weight of the water and the sky. It would be the sensible thing to think, but in the moments I could be drowning, I'm instead filling with determination. Just as I'm sure I'm making progress, someone grabs my arm and pulls me further down until we hit what I'm sure must be rock bottom.

It seems somehow less wet here, and as I contemplate how little sense that makes, I come to know that I am also breathing fresh air. I open my eyes to see the four of us are sitting in a house made from luggage. We didn't need to open it, we just had to arrange it so that there was space for us to exist among it! Annie pulls open the curtains and a sublime amber light streams in like we haven't seen in months. We all laugh out our relief, hard. As I open the door that takes us back to the square, I attempt to make a joke about how unlikely it is for Tommy to be the one forging new neural pathways, but he is already gone. We can only assume he's earned his way out of here.

A DEVIL OF EQUAL MEASURE

Ten white bulbs light up Sam's mirror, reminding him of the distant past. They used to be a symbol of new ideas, showbiz and vanity; now they mean only that he is preparing for yet another performance. He lays his foundation on thick to hide the bruises and, with silver powder on top, his face appears haunted by cracks and crevices. He paints blue diamonds over his eyes, and thick red lines around his lips to create an exaggerated smile. Natural smiles are long extinct.

Despite the sense of foreboding, there's something safe about the dressing room. The right to privacy before a show isn't often breached, so Sam can neck a few glasses of brandy and smoke a cigar before curtain call. The androids don't deny him those small pleasures, but they do prevent him from leaving the circus. He is a captive: a slave for their entertainment.

Sam does two shows every day. The first is a double act with a young android named Cody, in which he must mimic its sharp, angular movements and high-speed returning of mathematical equations. His inability to do either with accuracy is a source of hilarity for the androids, who make a guttural gurgling sound and rock back and forth in their docking stations surrounding the stage. Sam doesn't know whether the androids have genuinely developed a sense of humour, or whether they are simply demonstrating learned behaviour. He supposes that it makes little difference.

The afternoon show is the hardest. It is when Sam feels the most exposed; the most fearful of the two hundred sets of eyes, dead but illuminated, watching him in close-up. It is where the popularity of 'epic fail' and tasteless amateur stunt videos has come back to haunt humanity. Tasers, fast crashes, painful falls and confrontations with vicious wild animals are all regular features of the afternoon show, with Sam as the butt. He comes away with cuts, bruises, broken bones and tissue tears, and he fears for his life. Yes, he still fears for his life even though he knows that the androids will always repair him once they have had their laugh. Sometimes he wonders if this is the worse part; he will never be allowed to die, his career as a clown on infinite loop.

The androids don't seem to see the deterioration of his will to carry on. They understand only the physical aspect of pain, which they can treat. At least, this is how Sam desperately tries to think about it. The possibility that they know about his psychological suffering but use him as a toy for pleasurable cruelty is too much to bear. Then again, they did learn from the best. Where man attempts to create a god in his own image, he surely creates a devil of equal measure?

The buzzer sounds. Sam extinguishes his cigar, takes a deep breath, and waits to be escorted to stage left.

WE WERE NEVER TWO

The soft, red sand was overwhelmingly sympathetic to my sore feet. It had been quite some time since I had last been able to remove my shoes, but on that night my prince had insisted upon it. As always, he walked beside me: my rock, my guide.

The collar around my neck and leash he held tightly were almost invisible to us, but to any onlooker, we'd have appeared unusual to say the least. That attachment was my security, and the horns stemming from his temples were my protection.

The desert strip looked different at night. There were flaming torches casting shadows all around us, and it took me a little while to understand from which direction we were approaching the plain of the whispering wind. This was where the monster with the scythe lived and, having been through years of training with my prince, now was the time for me to face it.

He cupped my chin in his rough fingers. "Listen to

me. The only reason I have kept you leashed, and I mean the *only* reason, is that I didn't want you to get lost. You don't know these realms and your navigation would be inadequate, through no fault of your own. You're used to length and breadth and weight and time. None of those things exist here; they are at least two storeys below us in neuro-circuit terms, and there are countless beings ready to take advantage of your mind not yet being adjusted. Do you understand?" I nodded. He put his arms around me then, pulling me close. "My dear Florence, you are my strength."

Then I felt his fingers fumbling at the back of my neck as he unbuckled my collar and, soon after, a rush of cool air to the newly uncovered skin. My heart punched at my rib cage, and I very nearly choked on my gasp. I hadn't expected freedom to feel so much like fear. My eyes wide, I scanned the sands for him. It wasn't that he had disappeared, more that I could no longer grasp the sight of him. He was smaller than before, or I was bigger, or perhaps we were never two. I could hear his voice though, loud and clear.

"Fear, like sanity, must be overcome. It is an illusion that clouds your compass and prevents you from seeing things as they are."

The wind was picking up drastically by then so that I thought it might lift me right off my feet. I realised it was impossible to tell whether I had been standing upright to begin with.

"Fear is a force that guards the fence between worlds,

created by the monster with a scythe. It's something akin to an electrical current, or a sound wave only heard by humans and on a subliminal level. It hits you razor sharp in your amygdala to stop you approaching."

A strong gust scooped me right up then, and I was hovering above the desert sands. From up there I could see a long silver fence dividing the landscape in two. The other side looked no different, and yet that's where my prince seemed to be calling from. I longed to be there. I tried to direct my weight towards it, as though I could fly by imagination, but I was paralysed.

"That's the fear! Do you feel it? It's not real; it's an illusion. Cast it aside!"

Desperately I tried to ignore it, but it was eating me from inside. This was all unknown territory. I screwed my eyes up tight, and took five deep breaths as though I were about to head underwater. The fear is not real. Push through.

When I opened my eyes again, I was by the fence. It spoke to me in tall, graffitied letters: Are you sane? As I came closer, I saw myself reflected in its shiny surface, a caricature of a person, an image made from waves. A sneering female voice came now, "you don't belong here with us, just look at the state of you! Turn back, turn back, turn back!" The force of the words sent me flying backwards, and I got a mouth full of sand.

I felt naked and vulnerable, but I did not question whether the ordeal was worth it. Five more deep breaths. The fear is not real. As I re-approached the fence, I considered that the distorted mirror reflection was the real me. What was to say I wasn't looking back through the fence at myself from a place beyond time and space? What was to say I was ever made from atoms and not waves; to say my body ended where my prince's began? From then on, I deteriorated quickly. Tiny pieces of skin and hair crumbled away from me as though I were a sand castle kicked down by a child, and was taken by the elements.

I became a cloud of fragments, everywhere at once. I saw that there was no fence because I had been the fence. There was no prince because I had been the prince. The monster that slices everything in two: that was me too. I had created the very duality that plagued me. I had created segregation and separation from knowing the great All. Upon that startling realisation, I cast down my scythe, and in an instant, everything that had ever hurt me was nullified, along with everything else I had ever been.

THE THINGS WE DON'T REMEMBER

It's funny to think of all the things we don't remember. Like, I've been here in this world–or variations of it at least–for thousands and thousands of lifetimes, but I remember only choice segments of the last 21 years. Adrian says I'd remember more if I ever lived through something that made a deeper impression than my acrylic nails, but what does he know?

I do remember the day I met him. I was getting some fresh air in the park near my house, where a group of flexible fit freaks were doing yoga on the grass. He startled me, because I was scrolling through my news feed looking for a cat meme to share that would earn me enough 'likes' to keep me in with my peers. I didn't pay attention to the unusual in those days, since living was all about conformity. Adrian was totally peculiar. He slapped my phone right out of my hand and sent it skidding across the path.

"Do you know how much that cost?!" I yelled, diving

to pick it up in an attempt to minimise damage. Too late–the screen was smashed up, and the edges were scuffed. I wanted to cry, but my fury wouldn't let me, so I just resigned to my face growing red and puffed out hot air.

Adrian was laughing, hard. Some of the yoga girls were staring. A memory surfaced of the kids at school who thought they were better than me because they had the latest trainers. That was apparently reason enough to pull my hair and steal my lunch; to make me feel worthless. Cat memes weren't invented back then, so I hadn't been able to redeem myself. Instead, I spiralled into a black hole of fantasy.

Adrian held out his furry elongated fingers to shake my hand in apology.

"Come on, you can buy me a milkshake," were his first words to me.

My mouth dropped open. The hairs on my arms (that I didn't like to admit were there) stood on end. I lost grip on my phone and heard it clatter to the floor once again, because for the first time I saw that Adrian was a spider monkey. He was a huge one at that, looming two feet higher than me when stood completely upright.

"What's up? You look like you saw a ghost! Come on, I want my milkshake!"

"You're a… a…"

"Yes yes. Don't tell me you never noticed before?" I eyed him suspiciously. "Oh, come on. I see you literally every morning sitting on that bench gazing into your phone. You say hello to me most days!"

I started to back away, but not being used to moving backwards, or in fact looking where I was going at all, I crashed straight into a rubbish bin. Adrian burst into more fits of laughter.

I was furious at first, but then I began to laugh too: it was a mad situation, after all. At that point, I realised I hadn't actually laughed out loud in years (despite me continuously typing LOL on social media).

And then do you know what? I bought the monkey his milkshake. Banana. He slurped it down through a pink straw all in one go and burped at the end. No one else seemed to notice, and that made me feel special.

We chatted for a good couple of hours that day. He told me tales of what went on with evolution outside of the Internet, and about all the other things I couldn't remember. He told me I could still be an artist, if that's what I wanted, but I had to start looking directly at life. I cried, and he hugged me, and we agreed to meet again the next day.

"Pictures or it didn't happen," my peers said. Honestly, it hadn't even occurred to me to capture my new friend on camera. Maybe there was a part of me that feared they were right.

QUANTUM CONDUCTOR

Beneath the very particles of my being, I was waves all along. My position in space and time was a lie; permanence was only ever an idea.

We talk about wave functions collapsing to form objective reality, but that is upside down and inside out. A wave function does not collapse, it is merely that we (the observers) give birth to illusions based upon its pattern.

For man to think he creates reality by observing it, that he is essentially God to small things, is only true in a superficial sense. It is an ego's interpretation.

We perceive a reality we are equipped to understand. That is to say, a reality that makes use of the kind of sensory detectors we happen to have. A reality that shows objects to be at just one position in space and time at once: the position they are most likely to be in if they had to 'choose' given the data from all other things acting upon them. But outside of our minds, they don't have to choose. In fact, they don't have to obey measurement systems at all, they simply are.

Upon realising this, I have become a quantum conductor. I forget everything I think I know and allow the waves to travel freely through my fingers, to make music upon me, and I interpret the resulting pattern for man's instruments through my dance. I search for the part of me that conforms to the very essence of the music because I love how it makes my presence in the moment crumble. To be wholly at one with the harmony of the waves around us is to be attuned to all places at all times. It is to be connected to every possibility outside of the consensus reality tunnel, and as such, it cannot be accurately described, only understood.

To make something in wave form that is beautiful to us is the purest thing we can do because it reflects the illusions we have created back into the language of the infinite. A religious man might say it is like telling stories to God in her mother tongue. I say the music itself is the most meaningful thing we have.

COMMUTERS

It's a sad thing to join an underground train full of miserable, grey strangers who sit in half light and don't move or utter a single word to one another. That said, small talk is pretty dire too. So, on my way to work, I begin to think aloud.

"Hi there. Oh, you're reading Wuthering Heights! I'm haunted by the depth of emotion in that book; it got right into my heart and soul. Like when you see something so familiar that you had forgotten about for years and it all comes flooding back? It's a deep-seated memory in the unconscious. A memory that is ages older than all of us, and it makes you realise how small and insignificant you are as an individual, for humanity has been experiencing that animus projection myth for thousands of years. When you get down to myth level, you begin to realise there aren't nearly so many variations in experience as you had imagined."

I'm feeling shaky and panicked: negative in my mind.

I'm preoccupied with strange memories like being bored to tears as a nine-year-old and feeling tortured by a single song being on repeat and not being able to turn off the radio.

"This morning I woke up with Flunk's 'Queen of the Underground' in my head and I'll be hard pushed to shift it for the day now. But that's OK, I think. I feel like something terrifying is going to happen, something I am not emotionally equipped for. And I think whatever it is is going to be unavoidable. The only way out is through; my emotional state is temporary, tomorrow is a new day: I know all of that. But right now, I am stretched."

Come to think of it, all the songs I have listened to so far today have that 'darkness in the daytime' amber hue thing from my dreams. Perhaps I have not fully woken up. But I like it here. When will I ever access this beautiful feeling when it is appropriate?

"Appropriateness is the oppressor though, don't you think? There is comfort in discomfort. The paradox is king. My eyes are different shapes, maybe that is why I like things asymmetrical and unbalanced?"

I have fallen down a rabbit hole, that much is clear. What do these commuters make of me, I wonder?

"And all I get from my peers is an expression of their wanting me to come out and get back to 'reality'. 'Pull yourself together'. I hate that term so much. What if I'm happy here for a while, wallowing in my melancholy among the stars? Please let me alone. 'That's the illness speaking that isn't you!'. That isn't what you think is me.

But it's the version of me that produces all my best work and helps me to form a sense of centre and connection to the eternal."

I think of the term 'get a grip', and it reminds me of the long slender fingers with nails sculpted to a point I drew in art class once.

"Let's think of this as controlled madness. I have an anchor now. Or at least, I trust my guide and my inner self to the point that I know this is not madness. Or more accurately, this might be what you would call madness, but so long as it makes perfect sense to me, it is not too prolonged, and I don't allow you to see any part of it that might distress you, it is as good as any old sanity. Are you feeling distressed? I do hope not. You look nervous. I assure you I'm of no danger to you."

I'm no longer dipping my toe in, I know. I am swimming in the well. But my lady is here, and I see her as a beautiful deep indigo covered in tiny twinkly stars. And she is expressing that I am trained well enough to do this now.

All the commuters now look far away – thin sausage-like shapes in white. But I feel more like myself than ever before. I feel attuned and yet completely out of time with reality. This train and its seats look more and more dreamlike.

"There is always part of me that is ready to run away from the promise of money and comfort. And it has got to be that which puts me in this state. I think I'm lurking just beneath the accepted frequency of operation as I am talking to you now. There are very few lines and certainly no boxes. Does it seem like I have crossed a line to you?"

When I am feeling soulful in this way, or 'in a stormy mood' as my Mum would say, everyone in my proximity can feel the poison. Like a thick black tar is emanating from my mouth and creeping into every room, choking people and gripping their legs and paralysing them. It is quite an odd phenomenon because ordinarily I soak up the emotions and moods of others like they were my own.

"It is like I am literally inside out."

I catch my reflection in the window. *I have such a deep frown!* All my muscles are on auto while I sail off on this deep starry ocean. Believe me though; I am not in a place of terror. I will row my way back soon enough, with treasures I've no doubt.

"I think I'm in a surprise trance."

I hear a faint voice: *'bring it under control, this is a lesson.'* An alchemical image of the sun and the moon. I'm to move towards the sun now, aren't I?

'Take a breath
Feel your fingertips'
I drew them in art class!
'Rise at your station
Mind the gap'

"The good thing is that I'm feeling more and more in touch with my soul every day."

Rise at your station.

"There comes the point where you don't so much wish that certain things would come to pass, but you just

112

know that they will. Your will is aligned with that of the universe. So it's all good, I just need to learn to navigate these steep drops. Thanks for the chat."

Mind the gap.

In retrospect, I think as I head for the escalators, *perhaps the silence was preferable. It's quite a fine line between being friendly and being annoying, and another line between being annoying and acting insane.*

We must be careful of this thing they call sanity though; it's a tricky beast. It will have you turning grey and miserable. And worse than that, it will have you commuting.

BOTTLED UP

An old magician once told me that the essence of obsession is to be kept in small quantities on the top shelf. Its potency means it is to be used sparingly, else it will drag you right to the epicentre of your personal myth, where all semblance of the here and now will be lost.

"Beware the fool," he said. "It has been known to reduce people to a pool of nonsense with their soul detached and roaming. In such cases, the hope of administering an antidote is almost non-existent, and I'm sorry to say total implosion is the most likely outcome. But, if it works well, you will experience a creative boost for about three days after swallowing it. You will see the removal of your blockages and the fruition of your potential."

I took a tiny vial of the essence from him that day and put it on a shelf above my bed. I named it 'Alexander' after you, and put a label around its neck.

I didn't take the warnings lightly. I'd roll it around in my fingers sometimes, dreaming of the difference it could make to my life. But not until the day I received an eviction notice for non-payment of rent did I seriously think of using it. Blank pages had stared me in the face for weeks on end, and Mr Brown had had enough.

My therapist said I wasn't to think of you anymore. She said I had to 'break the cycle or break my mind', and she showed me how to reject the thoughts that contained you.

I loved you because you paid my bills and called me Empress. It's just a shame you were a devil. You used to beat me stupid, see. You used to pour liquid wax over me and make tiny cuts on my arm and grip my throat so I couldn't breathe. You used to scream until I shook and then tell me it never happened.

They took you away, but I never agreed to erase you entirely. My therapist protested. She said it wouldn't be healthy to merely blur your face: pixelation would only protect your identity and I would scratch at the scrambled squares like they were scabs. What use could that ever do?

* * *

Glug

"Rip out those stitches
Re-open my wounds
Tear another hole
In my heart

I don't want to see the world
Through frosted plastic
And fat bandages.
I want raw,"
cried the Fool.

"But never fully immerse!"
Warned the Magician.
"There's a sweet spot
And that is
where the art is"

"Just enough pain to inspire
Just enough sense
To turn it into something
That won't destroy me,"
reasoned the Empress.

S w a l l o w

* * *

My heart beat harder,
and images burst into my mind,
and a vein in my arm opened up,
and words began to squeeze their way out.

I…
Am…
Coming…
To…
An…
Understanding…

Then faster and faster they poured out so that I could no longer keep up with what they were saying. First clinging to my skin and then dropping down onto the carpet making a heap at my feet. I sank down to sit on my heels and examined them in handfuls. I rubbed my face in them. But there was no time, for my tiny room was quickly filling up, and I had to open a window so that I wouldn't drown.

The inflow of air was like a blank page. I was carried right out with the words on a wave, landing softly in the garden. Rising to my feet, I kicked through them like they were autumn leaves, and became giggling drunk on the euphoric air they were exuding.

Mr Brown came out to see what the commotion was. I expect he thought I had cracked up or was high on drugs, but when he saw the mountain of words on the lawn, his jaw dropped. At first, he picked one up and examined it as though it were a gentle snowflake, then started grabbing at more and more like they were £50 notes. I'm quite sure he saw them that way because if I could sell them, I would finally be able to pay up.

There'd be months of editing ahead of me now though,

trying to put all of those pesky words into the places they could shine brightest. I put up a meta grid around the house where I could post them into slots and rearrange them again and again until they bonded. And I put you back on the top shelf for a while.

FRAGMENTS OF PERCEPTION: THE MENAGERIE

I still have my notebook. By some miracle I am still without implants, upgrades and additional senses. However, I am in a small cage. It is only just tall enough for me to stretch my arms above my head and just long enough to take five comfortable paces. I have food, water, a comfy bed, and shelter. I have not been tortured as such, though it sure feels like it to be isolated from everyone I consider to be my species.

The unmanned helicopter that picked me up took me hundreds of miles across the sea and onto the European mainland. I'd practised my resistance speech all the way until the pod landed in an open field and I was greeted by a highly modified human. The genderless übermensch had puffed up synthetic cheekbones, violet eyes, and skin that glistened with a metallic sheen. They held their wrist up to a pad on the side of my vessel until it beeped and released me as though I had been bought and paid for.

They were visibly pleased to have me, their silicon lips

beaming and their arms gesticulating all over the place. It was obvious there was going to be a huge language barrier, in that all I got in exchange for my rehearsed words was grunts and clicks and pursing. I resorted to yelling expletives and lashing out with my fists, but was unable to get within a metre of my target without an electric shock hurtling through my torso. I tried to run but came against the same result, and fell to the floor clutching my chest. My host placed a hand upon their own chest, and blurted out what sounded like "Doc Schwarz". It is the only thing I have heard them say to this day.

When I was calmer, Dr Schwarz pulled me to my feet, and I had no choice but to be carried along by their side on an invisible current. They took me first into a conservatory full of exotic plants and birds. It was unbearably hot, but without a doubt the most beautiful botanic garden I've seen in my lifetime. I was reminded then of the lustrous hair my wife and daughter shared, and their eyes full of hope and clarity of mind. I ached for a moment but learned long ago that such yearnings are futile and don't give me the strength that will see me through. In the back of the conservatory was a door leading into a stone building held up by pillars: the place that has become my dwelling.

Inside there are several rows of cages like mine, varying in size to accommodate the broad range of animals in the collection. There are wolves, crocodiles, horses and chickens. There are even tigers, though I believed them long extinct. It is noisy, it smells bad, and I have lost track of the days I have spent here. Sometimes Dr Schwarz brings friends to come and look at me, most of them youngsters, and they take photos with their camera attachments. Such amusement they seem to get from my bald patch and the wrinkles forming around my eyes! Occasionally there are media drones, too. A truly natural human, it would seem, is quite an asset.

* * *

I write this now to beg for assurance that I have not lost my mind. The sound of the animals is both a comforting mantra to me and a source of endless torment. The visitors no longer come only in the daylight, but at night too. I can feel their eyes upon me in the dark as I try to sleep. It is different to being seen by the other animals; there's an indecipherable intent behind it. It is as though their eyes are seeing right through my skin and into my nervous system. I have nowhere to hide, I have no match for whatever it is that they are doing to me, and I have no proof that they are even real.

* * *

The tiger died the other day. A few hours later they brought it back, good as new but for a metal plate in its side. Why can't they see the suffering in the poor beast? My biggest fear is that they will do something similar to me when my time comes, and by heavens that must be soon. I'm losing hope of ever having something to do, of ever again being fulfilled and connected.

* * *

I have become dreadfully ill. I spend most of my waking hours coughing and vomiting; my eyes, ears and tongue are failing me. Dr Schwarz comes regularly and tries to administer a medicine which I refuse blankly. The media drones are now a permanent fixture by my cage; I assume they all want to capture the rare incident of a dying man.

It feels as though I am falling into the arms of a blissful eternity, where there are no sights and no sounds. I am outside of space and time, and I am outside of my body.

But wait; my wife is here now. She has changed, but it is her without a doubt. She is beckoning me, no, pleading with me.

"Take the medicine, Peter. You must take the medicine. It is the final filter, remember? It will give you the insight you need."

Her voice is soft, and it melts me. It has been so long since I heard the English language it sounds alien and yet safe all at once. And it is unmistakably her voice. How can that be?

"Join me, Peter. It's all over; you cannot win this by clinging on. Reality is shifting; you have to let go and be free. I can't see you like this anymore."

I am tired. I am weak. I cannot make sense. And then Dr Schwarz lifts me right out of the cage. I am losing my grip on the pencil; I'm afraid to say my body is out of my hands, and these words will be my last.

Did you enjoy the book? Please consider leaving a review on your favourite bookstore's website or social media pages. Thank you!

You can also connect with the author here:

Website: www.crdudley.com
Facebook: www.facebook.com/orchidslantern
Twitter: @orchidslantern
Goodreads: www.goodreads.com/CRDudley

ACKNOWLEDGEMENTS

This collection represents a year of writing short fiction, and as such the people who have inspired me are too numerous to list. I would, however, like to mention a few special individuals who have made publication possible.

First and foremost I'd like to express my sincere gratitude to Cy Dudley. Without his patience, support and encouragement this book simply would not exist. Cy has given me invaluable assistance in selecting, collating and formatting the stories, as well as entertaining many a conversation about the concepts that influenced them.

I'd like to extend a huge thank you to Paul Loughman, Phil Huston, Gavin Jefferson, Kenny Mooney and Mike Wood for helping me to make this collection the very best I could.

Thank you also to Natasha Snow for designing the perfect cover for the mood of the book, and for being an absolute joy to work with.

Finally, thank you to everyone who has ever made me question the things we take for granted as true; everyone who has encouraged me to dream, and everyone who has set challenges in front of me. You have all contributed to my colourful vision of the world as fragments of perception.

ABOUT THE AUTHOR

C.R. Dudley is a visual artist, writer, and mind explorer. She is fascinated by the human condition, in particular the effect future technological developments might have on the psyche, and sees everything she creates as part of one continuous artwork.

She started blogging in 2014 as a way to express the ideas stemming from her studies in Jungian psychology, philosophy and various schools of mysticism. Her first few stories were distributed as hand-stitched art zines in aid of a mental health charity, and her style became known for its multi-layered narratives.

In 2017 she founded Orchid's Lantern, a small independent press focusing on the metaphysical and visionary genre. She is the author of short story collection Fragments of Perception and a forthcoming series of novels inspired by VR therapy and the unconscious mind.

C.R. Dudley lives in North Yorkshire, and is a lover of forest walks, pizza, tequila and dark music.

Lightning Source UK Ltd.
Milton Keynes UK
UKOW04f1203281017
311767UK00003B/64/P